No 1
What I Do

No Matter What I Do

I END UP FALLING FOR YOU

Devanshi Sharma

Srishti
PUBLISHERS & DISTRIBUTORS

Srishti Publishers & Distributors
Registered Office: N-16, C.R. Park
New Delhi – 110 019
Corporate Office: 212A, Peacock Lane
Shahpur Jat, New Delhi – 110 049
editorial@srishtipublishers.com

First published by
Srishti Publishers & Distributors in 2017

10 9 8 7 6

Printed and bound in India

With the blessings of Radha Krishna,
without whom,
this book wouldn't have been possible!

Acknowledgements

A BOOK IN ITSELF IS MADE WHEN HUNDREDS OF WORDS PUT their effort together and each word becomes irreplaceable. That's exactly how each person in a writer's life adds to the writing experience. Starting with my parents, this book, or perhaps anything that I ever do in my life, is not possible without their endless and selfless support. They are my inspiration.

My grandparents, my family and my little cousins have been as excited for my writing as I have been. Giving me my space, always; it is difficult to be with a writer. The biggest reason that I can write with an open mind is my supportive and motivating family. If at all any book of mine has become a book from a manuscript, it's because of the endless support from them.

My childhood friends have been a great support, even when the book was prioritised above them at times. Thanks for not being nagging and the endless reviews, suggestions and chatter.

A special thanks to Miranda House that has given me an altogether new perspective. The beauty of the college lies in its independence. A big thanks to my teachers and friends in Miranda for helping me with reviews and synopsis.

Thanks to my office folks for being helpful and supportive. Every conversation regarding my writing means a lot to me.

I would also like to thank my Mithaas family, the little kids with whom I work. I thank each one of them for adding positivity to my life.

Srishti Publishers has been supportive throughout, and my deepest gratitude to the team there. 'Thanks a ton,' as my editor says (wink).

Prologue

MOUNTAINS – WHAT DO THEY REMIND YOU OF?

Calmness, tranquil breezes, serenity and a few days away from the hectic life of the city, right?

Urban landscapes are to a great extent responsible for the turbulence inside one's mind. Trust me if you will, the pace of a metro megacity completely exhausts you. There's just one word – run! Right from the first ray of the sun till the beam of the moon – run.

And it becomes all the more runn-atic when a person like me believes,

'*Late to bed, early to rise, makes one work wise.*'

And when twenty-four hours seem like twelve, then this saying is what I apply to myself. But, my grand mum always says, 'Excess of anything, howsoever positive, is dangerous.' My routine too, had become haphazard and monotonous. Every day – get up, get ready, get running, get going, come back, eat, watch TV, flirt with a few stories and sleep. A break was a must. And when I say must, trust me, it was absolutely – a must.

The world was just too complicated for me to stay for a few more minutes. *Saturation points – they keep coming and going, don't they?*

And so, throwing in a few pairs of shorts and t-shirts and my laptop into my bag, I decided to take the first bus to the hills. Why the hills, you might ask. The answer is simple – magnetic attraction.

After having visited Bharatpur and Mahabaleshwar, it was to be Nahaan this time.

What is Nahaan? Where is Nahaan? Why Nahaan?

A small town in the hills of Uttarakhand, Nahaan is not much known. Small places are left in the darkness of ambiguities at times. But, somewhere, I personally believe that small and unexploited landscapes are usually the places of self-interaction – it's where your conscience wants to open up and talk to you – free of all boundaries created by the world.

Ever happened with you, I wonder?

It was a similar journey for me. With a bag packed with excitement and thrill, I was all set to explore the hills of Nahaan. As the bus moved swiftly through the curves and angles of the hills, I started breathing serenity – such that I never felt before.

Wonder what the magic was.

Calm breezes brushed my face through the window. I deeply inhaled the air which was pure and uncontaminated with the materialistic pursuits of the brain.

And lo! Breathing the calm air, I never realized that the bus had reached Nahaan. I was to stay at one of our distant relatives' house. They had come to receive me and I could see them waving at me. I waved enthusiastically at my partners in crime.

Obvious a guess, is it not? My cousins!

As I got down, we shouted, screamed and marked the moment of our meeting with hugs and laughter. Until, one of them suggested, "Let's go home and relax."

Definitely not. Who sits at home when it was drizzling and misty outside! I turned down the idea and forbade anyone from returning home.

Magnetic attraction towards the woods, I assume!

And as always, domination helped me in convincing everyone to accompany me to the woods. I had heard a lot about them, thought why not explore a little?

Soon, we parked the car and walked towards the woods. As we walked ahead, the drizzle made space through the heavy fog. With every step that we took, the fog started building thick walls around us. While moving, we noticed hearts and arrows scribbled on trees. "Lovers point," my cousin pointed out.

We laughed in accord. But as my gang of cousins walked calmly, I don't know how and why, my feet started rushing towards the extreme left of the woods. The scenery was magnetizing and I was getting attracted towards the picturesque landscape. I didn't realize that I was losing contact with my cousins.

I kept walking and knitting a new story with the observations that I was making.

Stories were my date on such trips!

And dating one such story in my head, I didn't realize that I was far away from the world of people. I was alone and isolated amidst the beautiful landscapes. I walked towards the mist and the fog and ambiguities as they kept attracting me. I stood firm at one end of the woods which was succeeded by the depth of the hills. And strangely, I just kept looking blankly at the clouds. The breeze was rushing by while making the dry leaves dance and make creepy crackling sounds. I was all alone.

I felt a tap on my right shoulder. I turned immediately.

And you expect a ghost in a white sari? Old horror movies do that to our imagination.

Well...

A girl dressed in a denim short dress stood behind me. She gave me a bright smile. Her face was innocent and her eyes started narrating some details of an unsaid story already. She asked, wiping away my thoughts about her presence, "Too fond of stories, aren't you?"

Haila! I meet a girl three minutes ago and she knows I love stories. Sounds a little strange, doesn't it?

xii ★ *Devanshi Sharma*

I kept staring at her – blankly. Just as a child stares at the teacher.

Remember, when you had no answer to your teacher's question? Yeah! Just that.

The girl, like the smirking teacher gave me an 'I-know-everything' expression. I don't know why, but I felt like talking to her, knowing more about her and knowing about the story that she had in her heart, which her eyes had already started to narrate. And I – like a little kid, eager to know more about her, kept staring and listening to her as she started to narrate her first encounter with fate…

PS: My expression was more like a crazy cricket fan watching a crucial over in a match and as she started, I exclaimed on the fours and sixes, as I do when I watch a match with Dad at home. Ah, as always, I just can't stop comparing life with my favourite sport!

Well, the story was much like a nail-biting match, indeed.

Board meetings are supposed to be boring. Are they?

3:30 p.m.
23 April 2013
Conference Room, SVS Medical College, Bhopal

"MRS KHANNA, WE ALL HAVE IMMENSE RESPECT FOR YOU IN our hearts, but that cannot stop us from questioning your decision this time," said Mr Kumar. The head of administration and management in the SVS Institutions, Mr Kumar had been associated with the SVS group for the past seven years. He had never stood against any decision earlier, but played tunes of a rebel today.

He continued in his heavy voice, "Pardon me for my arguments, Madam, but the decisions you took in the past were genuine, unlike today's."

Another senior doctor, who sat with a taut and expressionless face added, "Absolutely, Ma'am. The love for your son has compelled you to take a partial decision like this."

The dignified lady reclined on her armchair. She studied the faces sitting opposite her. Dissatisfaction and annoyance was evidently visible. However, '*decisions, she thought, were the accumulation of permutations and combinations.*' Once taken, she didn't want to think much about them. She was the owner and the major shareholder of SVS Group of Medical Institutions, Bhopal.

Since 1988, she had parted with every joy in life to live this particular joy. She had sacrificed a huge chunk of happiness for her institute. She closely knew every brick of the college and had been constantly observant about the hospital.

And success had finally come to her. SVS was one of the best private institutions of the country today. And somewhere, Mrs Suhasini Khanna knew that if she could revive the institute from nowhere to the state it was now, she could certainly take the correct decisions even today. She was very stubborn about her decisions; perhaps an anarchist as well. And this was a fact which everyone sitting in the conference room knew already. She simply heard all the complaints and suggestions, after which she patiently waited for everyone to finish.

However, one voice which startled her was of Arun, her elder son. "Mom, I am a doctor earning lakhs in London. I am elder to Kushank and I deserve the chair. I thought you called me back to lead our business. But your decision shocks me."

Politics! Have you ever wondered how lice swiftly pass from one's head to another? Just a matter of spending some time together and in no time, you'll find the pest crawling in your hair too. Very similar to what is popularly known as politics. One might try to resist, yet one's surroundings can certainly affect one. And pests don't ask for your permission before entering your life, do they? Negativity is no different.

Arun was ambitious and his pride was clearly evident as he argued. Mrs Khanna was hurt. Any mother would be. She knew it was the pride and money which was speaking for Arun and not her upbringing. Still, she kept quiet. She wasn't a green horse. She knew that her decisions could make relations sour, but relations don't make institutions work, profit does.

Mr Das, a senior cardiologist spoke adamantly during the meeting, "Mrs Suhasini, you want a twenty-seven-year-old novice to lead all of us and tell us how to work? Madam, you must have invested your money in SVS, but even we have invested our time and devotion to take SVS to newer heights. Is this what we get for being loyal employees for the last twenty years?"

His words were ringing with ego, self-gratification and arrogance. Mrs Khanna undoubtedly acknowledged the fact that her team of doctors and professors had helped her sail forward. SVS had faced tough times initially and it was the core team which prevented it from sinking during the hard times. However, she could not agree to the fact that her decisions were being questioned, perhaps for the first time, and with such harsh words. She wasn't used to it.

The whole conflict, as it was clearly visible was that of position and power. Mrs Khanna, who had been the sole trustee of SVS, had decided to retire and transfer the responsibility of the college and hospital to her younger son, Kushank. It was indeed a strange choice when she chose Kushank over Arun. Arun was a doctor, and a good leader as well. His mother knew it.

On the other hand, Kushank didn't understand medicine; he was fond of business and management. He had a marketing brain. He ran an IT company along with his friend in Delhi which worked in App creation. Mrs Khanna was aware of the fact that Kushank liked working behind the lens where he just had to brainstorm marketing policies and sign on a few papers. He was afraid of leadership. In fact, he was under-confident to handle leadership. Despite all this, Mrs Khanna chose him to be the head of SVS. The choice was indeed atypical and therefore the ensuing chaos.

Anything apart from the usual creates strong waves in the ocean, after all.

Mr Kumar added, "Ma'am, forget about us, but think about your hospital. Ever since Kushank has started working, he has brought so many absurd ideas to the table. In the previous month, he admitted thirteen patients who were short on advance. In addition to it, he suggests loan payments. If this remains the graph, your business will run into bankruptcy one day."

"Absolutely correct. In fact, Suhasini ji, why don't you transfer all your responsibilities to Arun? He is certainly a better choice between both your sons," suggested one of the senior doctors loudly.

Arun's chest had broadened by a few inches, his expression turned more proud. Mr Das agreed, "Yes ma'am. Kushank doesn't have any experience and that is why he comes up with such childish ideas. He is a kid. Arun is perfect for the position."

As everyone finally gave a break to their endless complaints about Kushank and her decision, Mrs Khanna got up gracefully and started to walk out of the conference hall, without addressing anyone. Arun asked nervously, knowing his mother's temper, "Maa, we…"

Mrs Suhasini sharply replied to all the questioning eyes, giving a stern look to Arun, expressing her anger, "Thank you everybody for your suggestions, but knowing me well, you should have known that I believe in thinking *before* taking a decision. The meeting is over."

And she walked outside the conference hall. Arun was left gaping at his mother's 'insensitive' behaviour. However, it wasn't new to him. He had seen his mother being stubborn about her decisions – both personal and professional. He left disgusted.

On the other hand, Kushank was composed. He wasn't in the meeting, but he knew what the meeting was all about. The twenty-seven-year-old was smart and disciplined. He was still working earnestly, trying his best to understand the work. He was quietly looking at some reports from the hospital when he received an email.

It was admission time in SVS Medical College and being the new trustee, Kushank had introduced an email id which could connect him with the students.

I told you he had innovative ideas.

He had done this in his corporate office as well, to connect better with his employees. One email had just entered his inbox. It was written by an Amaira Roy.

Just then, Mrs Khanna walked inside his cabin. Kushank knew from her expressions that the meeting had been exhausting. He was aware that board members were not fond of him. He asked, sitting beside his mother on the couch, "Am I being too harsh or perhaps too...utopian, Maa?"

Self-doubt enters through constant criticism if self-confidence is dicey. In the past fifty days, Kushank had seen everyone unhappy with his working style and being the submissive self that he was, he certainly had doubts about his work. In Delhi, he gained confidence bit by bit as his decisions were innovative and profit oriented. But in Bhopal, that confidence was shaking. He had a desperate urge to go back to *his* world, where he wouldn't have to handle so many people.

The only herb that could cure his self-deterioration was his mother's trust.

Trust, they say, is a perfect medication for doubt.

Mrs Khanna knew that the journey was tough for Kushank, but she also knew that this journey could transform him. She explained, "Kush beta, fear is the only hurdle that you need to jump over. Be confident of what you are doing and stay strong. I trust your ideas and you know that I trust potential and not relations. Be correct and I'll stand by you always."

A mother is the only force which can re-shape, re-bond and re-build her child. One word of appreciation from the mother brings a plethora of positivity in life, and her support – well that's the priceless gift she provides us with. Kushank felt much stronger.

Kushank was a successful IIM graduate and was best comfortable in the corporate world. However, he had left behind his comfort zone for his mother. Mrs Suhasini had shown immense confidence in him and he could not let her down. He changed his world for his mother. Though Kushank knew handling the institute along with his own company was impossible, he didn't have the courage to leave his dream company either. He took some more time to rethink.

He was confused, doubtful and sailing in between his responsibilities and dreams.

Mrs Khanna got up to leave while saying, "I just know Kush that you are the sole person who caters to medicine as a 'service' and not as 'business'. You know little, but I am sure you'll learn. Arun knows a lot about medicine already, which will not leave space for learning. Be confident, child!"

Kushank smiled as he saw his mother walk away. He could see her trust, her confidence in him which was the sole reason he wanted to stay. For that pride in her eyes for him, leaving everything was worth it.

Careless

10:30 p.m.
23 April 2013
Bhopal

IT'S RAINING! IT'S RAINING! THE LITTLE GIRL IS PLAYING!

Weather is one of the most unpredictable forces on earth. Just like opportunities. When you crave for them, they make you wait and when they are least expected, they shower like blissful droplets. Even tonight, beating the scorching heat of Bhopal, rain had blessed the city.

But, blame global warming or the immense humidity, the rain that had started three hours back, didn't feel like taking a break.

Many people talked about how miserable it was to come home drenched, some blamed pollution and the changing weather trends, some parents ran to see to it that their naughty kids didn't run out in the rain, some cars struggled in the sluggish traffic and the list of woes continued. Everyone had a reason to talk about rain. Some love it, obviously. The lovers love it!

That night, rain had come without a cautionary warning in the month of April and was now being stubborn. It was frustrating for most people and Kushank was one of them. Like everyone, even he cursed the roads for being full of overflowing potholes and deep pits while he drove home. He missed noticing the beauty of the yellow reflection of the lights on the water. The dim street lights looked beautiful, only if they were appreciated.

One has to have appreciating eyes, after all.

Kushank certainly didn't. And cribbing never helps because it offers no solution. He was so pre-occupied with his thoughts that he missed the beauty around him. All he wanted was to be at home – within safe boundaries.

But that wasn't approved by the higher orders. When he saw the roads clearing, he started to speed up. But soon, he saw someone running from left to right on the road. He or she wasn't clearly visible to him in the thick rain, and before Kushank could realize who it was, he ended up inches away from hitting that person.

Because he pressed the brakes so suddenly, his car splashed water on the face of the girl who was running on the road. Kushank wanted to give her a piece of his mind, but as always, he did exactly the opposite of what he wanted to. He just started his car again until the girl, who was furious at him, walked towards his car and banged on the bonnet. He could partially see her in the dim lights – her hair dripping with water, her eyes sparkling with confidence, her face bright and full of changing expressions, and her persona strong. Kushank looked at her with gaping eyes when she banged on his bonnet again – louder this time.

"Come out. Now!"

She had a loud voice. Kushank didn't have an option but to step out of his car in the heavy rain. When he got down, he finally saw her clearly. In a pair of denim shorts and a tank top, she looked sizzling in the rain. Kushank could not stop himself from checking her out. However, she shouted back, "Don't you know how to drive?"

Kushank looked nervous. He didn't know how to react in such circumstances. He didn't know how to react to such confidence. But he looked at her and the object with which she was playing. It was a football. The girl, at midnight, in the rain, on the water logged-roads, was playing with her football and here she was blaming him for not driving properly. He struggled to gather some words and said, "But... It was your..."

He was sharply interrupted.

"Don't you dare say it was my fault. Because I know it wasn't. I was playing and my focus was on my ball. Your focus should have been on the road. So, apologize and leave."

She even defended her wrong doing so rightly that Kushank had to struggle for words, yet again. He thought, *Football at midnight, in the heavy rain and that too, alone. Interesting.*

Then he said politely, "Sorry."

"Join a driving school tomorrow," she ordered firmly.

He gaped at her with amusement. By now, he was enjoying looking at a creature like Amaira. After all, it wasn't regularly that he met such human beings. She shouted, "What are you looking at? Leave!"

And she threw her football back in the water and started playing again. Kushank looked at her through his rear view mirror.

With her wet hair, wide eyes and the swag that she carried, she looked smart and confident, perhaps slightly over-confident. He thought about her and continued driving. She had had an immediate impact on his mind; she was exactly what he always wanted to be – *carefree*.

Another left turn and lo! Kushank was home, back in his secure territory. He wiped the drops of water off his arms and wiped his mind of the desire of becoming carefree. *He was best as he was*, he thought and started browsing through some business newspapers. Being a doctor wasn't his cup of tea; he was a born businessman. And his mother had always supported his dreams, perhaps because she was confident of him more than he was of himself. Kushank was a partial introvert and an under-confident human being. He needed to be pushed. Perhaps this was not something he wanted himself to be involved in. He wanted to see himself just like that girl in the rain. He wanted to be her, instead of being what he had become.

Kushank didn't like expressing his feelings and opinions, but the girl in the rain was overflowing with expressions and strong opinions. She was playing unconcerned in rain until a voice called her name.

"Amaira. It is Kabir."

She turned and saw her aunt waving at her. Had it been anybody else in the world, Amaira wouldn't have cared to go back home, but Kabir was the only key which worked with this lock. She ran back, drenched with water and her football in her hand. Her aunt gaped at her as she took the call.

"Kabir! You just disturbed my football session. I'll call you later," she said briefly.

Kabir sternly said, "Amu, you are going nowhere. I hope you remember that you are not at home."

"So? Football is not restricted just to home, Kabir. And how does it make a difference?" she retorted.

"Of course it does. You went to Bhopal for filling admission forms, not to play football at midnight. Don't make a nuisance of yourself at Kavita aunty's place, Amu," he explained.

"What nuisance yaar, Kabir? I am just playing. Aunty doesn't have a problem. She is cool. In fact, you should be like her."

"But I have a problem. Dry yourself right away and go to bed. Come home and play all night, I won't say a single word. Understand?"

She didn't say anything, but Kabir carried on, "You better sleep now; you have a flight to catch early in the morning."

"Kabir, just tell me one thing before I go. Will you?"

"What it is, Amu?"

"Were you a jailor or Hitler in your previous life?"

And smirking, she kept the phone down.

It was obvious from the conversation that the siblings were best at fighting.

Remember how many times you have fought with yours?

Amaira was uncontrollable and Kabir was her mentor, perhaps partner in crime. Kabir was just two years elder to her, but his maturity was way ahead. With a childlike Amaira, the guardian naturally becomes mature. Kabir, in one word, was 'everything' for his sister, and Amaira was, in return, the world to her brother.

Isn't it the case with most lovable siblings? They fight, crib, cry and in some extreme cases, also hit each other, but at the end of the day, they are the closest to each other!

The journey back home!

6:05 a.m.
24 April 2013
Raja Bhoj Airport, Bhopal

"HAVE A SAFE FLIGHT *BETA*. AND COME BACK SAFELY," KAVITA
aunty said.

Parting at the airports is usually an emotional task for relatives
and friends – out of will or not is debatable though. Kavita had met
her niece after such a long time and she was happy, barring a few
things. On the other hand, Amaira was ignorant about the affection
her aunt gave her. For Amaira, it was all too formal. Since childhood,
she had only seen her mom, dad and grandparents. That was the
definition of a family for her. She didn't understand other relations.

Amaira smiled formally saying, "Sure aunty. Thank you."

She had her own space at home. When she went to stay
somewhere away from home, she felt as if she was denied her space.
In fact, she was happy that she was going back. At least she could
keep her half-eaten apples on the table or unwashed clothes on the
bed. She walked past the security check and reached the waiting
area briskly.

Bhopal is a comparatively smaller airport than the one in Delhi.
The flight status was displayed on the screen and unfortunately for

12

the ground staff, her flight was delayed by two hours. Being the impulsive girl that she was, Amaira walked to the airline's counter. Her theory was: when anger strikes, do anything but find someone you can vent it out on. The poor chap at the counter was the butcher's goat, it seemed.

As she stood in front of the counter, the well-dressed man asked humbly, hospitality overflowing with his words, "Yes ma'am? Is there anything I can help you with?"

"Of course. It's 7 a.m. already. When is the pilot planning to fly the plane Mr...?" She checked his name on his shirt and continued, "Mr Khurana."

Yet again, a nasty passenger right in the morning, the man thought. He explained, "Ma'am, we are really sorry for the inconvenience caused. It had been raining heavily last night, due to which we had to delay all our flights..."

Amaira interrupted him. "Because of which my flight will be an hour or two late, right?"

She was impatient. The man pleaded politely. "Ma'am, we will try our best. Please bear with us."

Amaira thought for a moment and then smiled. "That's fine. I know it's not your fault. But could you compensate for the time I am losing right now?"

The man looked puzzled. This girl was playing with words. The man felt irritated. For him, Amaira was just a youngster making a fool of him. However, he was taught to tolerate and accept anything that he was served by the passengers. He maintained his calm.

"Ma'am, pardon me?"

"Compensation? Why don't you give me a chance to fly my flight? Then, I would have no problem sitting here for four more hours."

The man on the other side of the counter almost froze. He had handled a lot of stubborn passengers, but Amaira was unpredictable.

His perception of 'youth' initially made him judge Amaira as a nasty, 'spoilt' brat, which wasn't completely untrue. However, she was a very different person from what she appeared to be.

She was complicated, to say the least.

One moment he thought she was making a light-hearted conversation, the other minute she was sarcastic. He was tired of trying to make out what she wanted until she laughed a bit, saying, "Sorry. I was kidding. One needs to pass time at such boring waiting lounges, you know! But yes, the offer is still open. Ask your airlines, Mr Khurana."

In one minute, his perception changed. She was now a youngster who had a 'good' sense of humour. He smiled at her as he saw her walk away from the counter. Amaira winked and went towards the food shops. Foodie – that was the exact adjective to complement this noun. After looking around for about twenty odd minutes, Amaira bought a vegetable wrap, a coffee and a chocolate brownie, and walked towards the windows from where she could see the airplanes taking off.

Height always fascinated her.

She sat and started to bite from the wrap. While eating the not-so-tasty junk food, Amaira saw her phone buzzing. It was one of her school friends.

"Hey Sharad! How have you been?"

The voice from the other end replied, "Forget about me, Amu, I just heard you cleared the entrance for SVS. I must say girl, you are so lucky."

"Being lucky is never Amaira's cup of tea, Sharad. Hard work pays at the end," Amaira replied, taking a bite from her brownie.

"Of course. I just called to congratulate you. So, when are the classes starting?"

"In three weeks," she replied.

And just when he was about to ask something, the airlines

made an announcement. Amaira got the perfect chance to cut the conversation short. She hurried, "Hey, I really got to go Sharad. Will catch you later. Bye."

The announcement was obviously not for the departure of her flight, but Amaira's thoughts had been going haywire for the past few days. It was two years ago that she had decided to become a doctor. A month later, she joined the best coaching institute in Delhi, and a year later, she was struggling and juggling between school and coaching. Three months later, she was studying rigorously for the entrance exams and a month later, she found out that she hadn't cleared the AIPMT. The next thirty-six hours were spent in endless questions: 'What if you can't make it to any college? What if you've flunked SVS too? What if AIIMS doesn't work out?' Many negative thoughts clouded her until five days later, when she checked the results of SVS college.

Although a private college, SVS was transparent about their admissions and was considered to conduct one of the tougher entrances. But, once she cleared it, she was on cloud nine.

Crunch.

She took a bite of some of the crunchy chips which accompanied the vegetable wrap. And the sound of the bite brought Amaira back to the present. She smiled looking at the aircrafts which took off. She calculated the transition that an aircraft made from land to the sky. She smiled as it seemed quite like her admission to college. A couple of days ago she was ecstatic about her flight to Bhopal and had made a hundred calls back to Geneva to tell her parents about the minutest details. She had stopped Kabir from leaving the house, she had updated her status thrice before leaving and she hadn't spent a moment without a smile. And a day later, she was in the flight waiting for that transition!

❖

9:45 a.m.
A Day Earlier
SVS, Bhopal

"WELCOME TO RAJA BHOJ AIRPORT. THE TEMPERATURE outside is thirty degrees. We hope you had a comfortable flight and would give us a chance to fly with you again. Have a pleasant stay at Bhopal."

The confident airhostess announced as the aircraft landed in Bhopal. Amaira, brightly smiling on the very thought of entering a new zone, impatiently got up to leave. Seeing her get up, the good looking flight attendant hastily requested, "Ma'am, please be seated. The seat belt sign is still on." A forced and formal smile accompanied the attendant.

Most of the time I travel, I find some passengers jostling to get out as soon as the plane lands. Honestly, I have always thought them to be impatient and restless, but I never thought about it from their perspective. Perhaps, they were eager to start a new journey and every second seemed like an age. Like it was with Amaira.

However, only she knew the reason for her excitement. For the crew members, she was just an impatient and restless passenger. How would they know Amaira was still in the sky?

Anyhow, Amaira smiled sheepishly and sat down. Meanwhile, her eyes had checked out the steward and had silently marked him as 9/10. Ah! The root of this habit goes back – way back.

Amaira restlessly waited to reach her new college. Wasn't it like the first day at school? Everything had already happened in her imagination – she had imagined a lovely college life with all the little things that accompanied it. She wanted to live them out now.

As she waited, she took out her phone and texted Kabir. Every moment increased the force with which her heart thudded.

Soon enough, she was walking confidently out of the airport. Kavita aunty had sent her driver to pick Amaira up. Amaira sat in the car and greeted the driver, as if she had known him for ages, "*Bhaiyaji, sab badhiya? Ghar pe sab theek?*"

Some peculiar traits never fade off. Amaira could be friendly to anyone – and in spite of the fact whether she knew them or not!

The poor driver, not knowing how to respond, just smiled and nodded. Amaira called Kavita aunty and formally informed her, "Aunty, the driver was here. Thank you."

"No need for that, *beta*. Come home for breakfast and then I'll accompany you for your *admission*."

Amaira immediately replied, "No aunty. Please don't bother. I'd like to go to the college first. Do you mind if I get my admission done first?"

The lady on the other end was hesitant. She thought an eighteen-year-old needed a guardian. She insisted, "Amaira, it's just a matter of ten minutes dear. Our house is very close to your college."

"But aunty, losing ten minutes means a precious loss of six hundred seconds. I'll just get done with the formalities and then we'll party together. See you."

She didn't even let her aunt speak, and left poor Kavita aunty waiting for her niece at the dining table. She judged Amaira as a stubborn kid even when she tried hard to not be judgmental. Amaira gave her all the reasons, she thought.

Meanwhile, Amaira called Kabir, who was fast asleep. She called twice, thrice and finally he picked up after the fourth time. Amaira snapped, "Your sister is getting her admission, you lazy bum. Get up!"

"Amu, relax a bit. I was tired after dropping you at the airport and college union work is getting the…"

"Shut up Mr '*I am Kabir*'. And you better not make arrangements without letting me know. Why did you ask Kavita aunty to come with me?"

Kabir smirked. He had expected a similar reaction. He replied in a sleepy tone, "I just thought you'd be well acquainted then…"

"Shut up. Don't tell me that you accompanied me everywhere I travelled in Delhi. Come on, I am eighteen. I am an adult. Now, go back to sleep. I'll call you after getting my admission done. And call mum and dad too. Bye."

And she hung up. Again, without letting Kabir complete his sentence. Kabir smiled at her and went back to sleep.

The driver stopped the car outside a magnificent gate, of course not as opulent as those mythological palaces, but eye-catching for sure. Amaira got down with her documents.

Quite dramatically, Amaira saw a motion movie in her head when she stepped inside the gates. Just as they showed in movies, she saw herself entering a new world.

Just like the first episode of a daily show starts, Amaira saw herself entering a new regime.

She smiled at herself and felt the atmosphere around her. And just as she stepped and looked towards her left, she saw the most beautiful part of the college – the green sprawling lawns.

Just like the lead of the serial looks around in awe.

For once, Amaira jumped with excitement on seeing the lawns. She was so impressed by them. The beauty of the college lay in the lawns – huge, square-shaped and mesmerizing. Beautiful was the only word which could define them. However, as she walked ahead, Amaira saw the college building. She had not expected it to be so old and trite. Not as glamorous as they portrayed colleges to be in movies. Amaira melodramatically turned towards the lawns and silently compromised with fate. *Dramatic, she was.* All this while, she constantly chatted with her brain.

Remember the voice which runs behind in the background? Yeah. That!

She was unaware that she was being closely observed by the senior students. Amaira's persona, her swag certainly attracted eyeballs. But, did she even care? She simply walked ahead, without turning back.

When she reached the office, she was even more disappointed. The Bollywood movies never mentioned over-crowded offices in colleges, she thought. 'From where will a student get the idea of standing in long queues?' She shook her head in silent despair of the broken expectations. SVS was a renowned college and it was supposed to be well-equipped. Melodramatically, yet again, she thought of the open lawns and tried to console her disappointed heart.

She sighed as she walked towards the office.

The office was buzzing with a swarm of students. Everyone wanted to go first. Few were quarrelling, some were exchanging obscenities in frustration and the rest were pushing and pulling each other. And in between this, the office staff was indifferent and rude. Amaira initially got into the long queue and tried to remain patient, but after standing for thirty-thirty five minutes, she excused herself and walked to the clerk sitting there. She said, "Sir, the queue is not moving ahead at all. It's been thirty minutes. Kindly arrange an alternative."

Wasn't that polite?

The clerk retorted, looking at her through his round geeky glass frame, in an ignorant tone with a scowl, "This is the way we work. If you have a problem, then you are free to leave. Now, get back in the line."

Amaira's blood boiled with anger, but she gulped it down. She knew getting into an ugly spat of words on the very first day of college could be dangerous for her. She quietly got back to her place, but just after ten minutes, she saw the office staff getting up for lunch. Amaira's patience was slowly giving up. She requested again, "Sir, we have all been waiting since an hour and it's humid. Please quickly finish the formalities."

She got a sharp answer. "Madam, we are human, we need food to work. Please go."

Amaira again went back into the line, trying to be patient. But as she turned, the clerk commented, "These rich kids want everything served on their plates."

The comment was loud enough to be heard by Amaira. She clasped her fist tightly as she was losing her patience. She didn't know how to vent her anger and on whom. *Keeping quiet*, she thought was *just not her way*. She wanted to sharply revert but she swallowed her anger. And just when she was thinking of slapping and punching the man, her eyes read a notice: 'If anyone has any complaint against the staff or teachers or any student in the college, write it to us. We will hear you out.'

'If you have a problem?' she exclaimed loudly in her mind. How enthusiastically she wanted to narrate all the problems that she had. She took out her phone to type the mail. Get a reality check, Mr Khanna, she talked to herself while typing the brutally frank mail.

Dear Mr Khanna,

It is quiet ironical to see this notice outside an office where nobody cares to listen to the students. I just reached the city from Delhi. The lawns are beautiful. The infrastructure is average but because this will be my college in a month, I'll try to love it. It is one of the best private institutes of our country, but the way things work here is unfortunately startling. Since the morning, I have been standing in this unending queue and so has everyone else. The office has just one counter operating for two hundred and forty applicants. The staff needs to go for loo breaks, lunch breaks, tea breaks and every possible break in the world. At five, I am sure they'll shut the window on our faces and will say 'Come tomorrow'. I was just confused, are we potential doctors or salesmen? I was angry and irritated and didn't know where to vent my anger, so channelized it by writing to the owner the college.

I haven't met you, but would love to meet you, sir. Because I have more things to say. I hope my suggestions don't result in my expulsion from the college even before admission.

(And I will certainly not hide my identity. If I haven't done something wrong, why should I fear?)

Amaira Roy.

And it was after pressing the send button that Miss Roy finally took a relaxed breath. And finally, after waiting for long and some more arguments, the staff managed to complete her admission. Finally, she was a part of SVS.

Once she was done with the formalities, she called Kabir and exclaimed, "Kabir! I am done with all the formalities. Your sister is a potential doctor now."

Kabir smiled broadly and whispered back, "Amu, I am in a union meeting; will call you in a while. Bye."

And he hung up. The only point that these two made was to always make sure that they picked up one another's call. Howsoever busy Kabir may ever be, he would never miss Amaira's calls.

His score of 97% in his CBSE boards had landed Kabir in one of the best commerce colleges of India. He was pursuing a degree in Economics Honours from SSRC, the best commerce college of Delhi University. He studied insanely hard. However, another side of the same person was his increasing interest in politics. He had, in fact, been elected as the vice president of their union. Since then, his classes had taken a back seat and all that mattered to him was to be prominent in the union and fight the DUSU elections sooner or later. He was active in all the party meetings and events. And of course, being an active member in the union brought him into the limelight, which he enjoyed. The idea of being the centre of attraction always fascinated him. He liked the hectic social life.

Nonetheless, he took measures to make sure he was what he wanted. *Ambition, it seemed was running in the blood of the Roy family!*

After calling Kabir, Amaira texted her mom and dad. Preeti saw the text and smiled broadly. Akaash was equally happy. And it was now that Amaira could eat to her heart's content at Kavita aunty's place.

"The flight for Delhi is ready for departure. All passengers are requested to proceed for boarding through gate number two."

Amaira's flight was all set to take off. She quickly gathered all her scattered thoughts and got up to leave. While leaving Bhopal, she had dreams, thoughts and aims which were new to her. She wanted to live a new journey, live a new adventure in life.

In the next fifteen odd days, her life would be turning a full 360 degrees. This thought brought a little smile on her face, but hidden behind the smile was a pinch of worry. But her excitement overcame the worry in no time. While wondering, imagining and day dreaming, Delhi arrived.

PS: Not to forget, while checking out a few 'good' co-passengers and stewards.

Amaira took a taxi from terminal three and reached home. Kabir had was not yet back from college.

Amaira was independent and self-reliant. In fact, both Kabir and Amaira were brought up as confident and independent young siblings by their parents. Akaash and Preeti had been ambitious workaholics, but even before that, they were good parents. Both of them never had the freedom of choice before they got married. Even though they belonged to South Delhi and were from rich households, they never stood alone as Akaash or Preeti, but were someone's kids or someone's descendants, until they took a dive into their dreams. And they both knew that only independence had given them the power to build the world they were living in. They had started a restaurant chain and were pursuing the life they always wanted to – independently.

Then, how could they not imbibe the same independence in their children. They brought up their kids as friends and as independent individuals. Amaira was a product of such upbringing – of course with a tadka of her own style.

Now you know why Amaira was Amaira?

Once she got home, Amaira opened the lock with the spare key that she always carried and as soon as she entered the house, she impatiently connected a video call and spoke to her parents. She couldn't live if she didn't tell them everything that had happened in her life. Akaash was evidently a proud father, who said, "Amu, congratulations dear. You make both of us very proud."

"I know, Papa. Where is Mom?"

"She'll be here in a minute. There was a client who had to be handled. Let her be."

Akaash winked. Amaira winked back. She said, "Poor client. Mom will be so —"

Preeti entered the room upon hearing the father-daughter conversation. She said, "Amu, you and Akaash just need a reason to make fun…"

"Mom, relax. We love you too!" Amaira smirked. Akaash gave her a winning look. Truly, Amaira was her daddy's princess. In fact, both Akaash and Amaira had trillions of things in common, including the fact that they couldn't move a step ahead without Preeti.

Parents are the first friends that we make. Be it our stubborn attitude in teenage or workplace stress, they are the only people who can handle us best. And until the happiness is shared with them, life can never be happy.

Coming back to the conversation, Preeti said, knowing the duo, "Anyway, you tell me Amu, how is the college?"

Amaira replied with a disappointed expression, "It doesn't match up to my expectations. I was too excited – but it looks a little dull. Except the green, open lawns. They have the perfect amount of sunlight, shade and breeze. The open is far better. I am sure I am spending the next five years sitting under some trees in the lawn. Who knows Mom, I might become an enlightened figure in the next five years and you'll come to meet me under those trees to seek my advice some day."

She broke into laughter. Her parents smiled as well. However, they tried to explain to her the practicalities of life. *It wasn't a Bollywood movie after all.*

After chatting for an hour, Amaira concluded narrating her first impression and the 'adventure' she had had. Akaash encouraged her actions saying, "That's good. Even that trustee should know how stupid the employees in his college are. In fact, I think even I'll write to him."

Preeti looked at him with a frown and then turned to Amaira, saying, "Have you lost it, Amaira? You better keep a little calm in the new atmosphere. You should be a little careful."

Mothers are always protective about their children. And Preeti was a practical mother. She had read many stories about ragging in medical institutes and Amaira's attitude had started becoming a matter of concern for her. She couldn't encourage her daughter to rebel under such conditions. She knew that rebellion brought risks. She was scared for her daughter.

However, Akaash said, "Of course not, beta. Just be yourself. And I am sure, you'll handle everything. You are Amaira. Just be vigilant Amu, that's it."

Preeti and Akaash were sure to have a little argument over Amaira. Amaira's anger was hereditary from her father, whereas Preeti, the much mature between the two had most of her impressions in Kabir. That was perhaps the reason why both Amaira and her dad needed Preeti and Kabir desperately. As they say, two halves make one complete.

Hi Kabir!

7:15 a.m.
Rang Bhavan, Gurgaon

"RAMESH, HOW MUCH TIME MORE? I'LL GET LATE FOR college. I have an eight-forty class." Kabir asked anxiously. He was an early riser and had quickly got ready in his casuals. But he was getting late because of their cook who was still cooking. Amaira never woke up early. She never needed to. Kabir handled everything – perfectly. Wasn't he genuinely too good!

Ramesh, their cook replied hastily, "I had already made the food on time, but Amaira didi told me to make red sauce pasta for breakfast. It takes time, bhaiya."

Kabir, clearing his square-framed spectacles, sighed and walked to Amaira's room in exasperation. He banged open the door and saw Amaira reading the Page 3 news casually. At times, she was synonymous to the word irresponsible. Seeing Kabir, she greeted him with a yawn, "Good morning. Why are you looking so terribly right in the morning, Kabir?"

"Because you are impossible Amaira! At seven in the morning you want to eat red sauce pasta. Seriously?"

He was about to snap at her again when his phone rang. It was Raghav, his best friend.

"Raghav, you go ahead. I'd be late for the first class. My sister wants to eat pasta right in the morning. I'll get late."

Amaira looked defensive. She retorted while he was still on the phone.

"How dare you? Kabir, did I tell you to wait till Ramesh bhaiya leaves? Get lost. I haven't stopped you. All of a sudden you want to attend morning classes today. Cribbing about a sweet sister - ALWAYS."

Kabir retorted, by now completely forgetting about Raghav's call, "Yes, of course. The sweetest, I must say. I should leave you? You very well know I don't leave you alone with anyone at home. I am scared for them, after all."

Raghav, who was used to overhearing these morning wars over the phone, silently disconnected the call. He turned to Anuriti and said, "We'd better leave Anu, he'll join us later. Let's rush, Madhavi won't let us enter the class otherwise."

Madhavi Chitti was one of their strict professors.

"Amaira is back, is she?" Anuriti inquired laughing.

"Indeed. She is back and is having pasta in the morning."

Anuriti and Raghav chuckled and boarded the metro for Vishwavidyalaya. Anuriti and Kabir had been childhood friends and Amaira had always been part of all their tantrums. It was because of that bond, that Anuriti knew Amaira so well.

Back at home, Ramesh finally prepared the red sauce pasta and left. Kabir then told Amaira at ten past eight, "Amaira, I am leaving. Have your lunch and if you are planning to go out, text me. And take the money from the drawers."

"Stop lecturing me, Kabir. I know everything. Have a good day."

And it was with a smile that the siblings waved goodbye to one another. Kabir rushed down the stairs of their bungalow and took an auto from the nearby auto-stand. It was the month of April, when exam tension starts building up in DU. Kabir was a little worried – though by now he had stopped worrying about his grades, he sure wanted to pass. Some way or the other, he knew he would sail through. While the auto driver drove, Kabir's ruffled hair started becoming more ruffled and he adjusted them with his fingers and fiddled with his mobile phone.

The last few classes for the current semester were remaining. Perhaps those were the only which he attended with such devotion. He paid the auto driver and ran inside the metro station to catch the metro. Making his way through the chaotic crowd, he caught the train.

That's what happens when you have a sister like Amaira at home.

❖

3:30 p.m.
Canteen, SSRC

APRIL, I TELL YOU, IS ONE OF THE HOTTEST MONTHS IN DELHI, and in between the harsh heat, the classes completely saturate one's desire to do anything else in life. After attending such exhaustive classes, all one aspires to become is a sloth, who sleeps for twenty hours a day!

Phew! That's what exams do to us.

Anuriti was sitting at one of the round tables of their well-built canteen, along with a few classmates. They were cribbing about random things – from teachers to syllabi, from studies to presentations, from this to that, from nothing to everything. The aroma of freshly-fried Chinese food had filled the canteen as the girls chatted. She was sipping from the chilled ice tea while talking casually when suddenly Kabir walked to the table and shook the round table top, startling Anuriti.

"What the—? KABIR, I'll kill you someday!" she shouted.

He smirked and pulled Anuriti out of the canteen. He said, "We are going to Book Land. There are some guides which will help me pass this semester."

Anuriti replied, "Guide books? Come on, you'll pass as it is."

"Babe, one needs to know what's in the syllabus to pass. Come. Raghav will accompany us from the gate."

Chatting and eating, they bought the books and ran back home. Kabir hated this time of college. He loved working over budgets, running around for arrangements and gracefully stealing the limelight at the end of his successful endeavours. He liked attending party meetings and protests. Exams were just not his cup of tea. He was ambitious in another field.

Well Kabir, all we can say is that just like the other phases, this too, shall pass.

Anti-clockwise

12:07 a.m.
17 May 2013
Kushank's cabin, SVS, Bhopal

TIME, IT IS SAID, IS ONE OF THE WEAPONS OF THE SUCCESSFUL.
Life gives you opportunities, but it is time which decides whether
the chance stays with you or not. In the course of harsh times, it is
in staying firm that a winner is created. Kushank faced innumerable
criticism at the beginning of his journey, which if I say didn't affect
him, would be untrue. He was definitely affected, but Mrs Khanna's
support kept him going. At the same time, his heart was desperately
craving to go back to Delhi. But every time he saw his mother's
unconditional trust, he couldn't tell her how much he didn't connect
with her institute. In fact, the trust made him work harder for the
hospital. His mother's belief in him was the sole reason which kept
him bonded with Bhopal.

Reclining on his chair in between scattered files, Kushank
gathered all these thoughts. He was a hard working man, which
made him stay wide awake till midnight. At the same time,
inspections were round the corner and with the dirty work place
politics around, he didn't trust anyone but himself. While he was

working, his phone rang. It was Vishesh, his business partner. Kushank picked up the call expecting some kind of a relief from that end, but Vishesh sounded drunk and started to attack him, "Kushank Khanna, are you even planning to come back... or our business will drown? I will get des... destroyed."

At least three or four glasses of scotch would have been needed to get Vishesh drunk, Kushank thought. He knew there was no point arguing or explaining at that moment, but silence made things worse. He heard the sound of breaking glass. Vishesh must have broken the glass bottle on the floor.

Kushank asked, "Where are you right now Vish?"

"In hell. Why do you have to care you, bloody selfish man? You are rich; go eat on that. Let me at least drown in peace."

Kushank understood Vishesh's anger. He knew what their company meant for his friend. In fact, they had started earning profits after a harsh struggle and when success arrived, Kushank had to leave. Coincidently, losses knocked again and the graph which had started rising started to go down. Vishesh had invested all that he had in his business. He had married a month ago and expenses in the tough city of Delhi had started haunting him. The timing of events was such that Vishesh blamed Kushank for leaving the company mid-way.

Kushank, on the other hand, knew well that he had left the boat in turbulent seas. But, he was enmeshed. When he heard Vishesh being abusive, he didn't have an option but to keep the phone down and to concentrate on the files he was studying. He was working out the rates and accounts of the equipment deals. The labs were in a trite condition and the first big project which Kushank took in his hands was to renovate the labs. It was a deal worth lakhs and taking right decisions was mandatory for him, especially when he had to prove to the board that he, if not a true leader, was at least a good decision maker.

He had rechecked every transaction with his accounts team and made sure that each paisa had a record in the accounts. He didn't wish to fall prey to any controversy later, so he tried to be doubly sure before investing.

He checked the equipments and the list of the dealers which the lab staff had submitted to him and kept a close watch on the rates, even tallying them online.

Money matters were always crucial for a businessman.

However, his head had twenty drums banging inside. Tired and exhausted, he looked at his watch. It was 1. Kushank wanted a coffee but knew the fact that nobody apart from him would be around in the college. And he was too lazy to get up. At the same time, going against the will of his mind, he had to work and place the order by the morning. Time was less, work was more!

Ah! And I had believed that we work best under pressure. It was so untrue for Kushank.

He read the file of the biochemical lab, which had an expenditure of twelve point five lakhs, but when Kushank figured out some exaggeration in the list, he decided to check the details himself. He got up and walked out of his cabin, walking towards the lab. As he walked ahead, the baffled guard came running towards him. He asked, "Sir, you – here?"

He looked terrified. Nobody took a round at this hour, except the wardens, and they, well never turned up. For the first time they had the owner of the college taking a note of the lab at such an hour. The guard started being nervous.

Kushank asked, "Is the lab locked? Give me the keys."

Raghu, the guard started fumbling.

"S-sir... b-but"

Kushank could see beads of sweat on his forehead. All of a sudden, Kushank could smell trouble and whenever he heard the word 'trouble', he started to lose his mind. He started getting panicky and insane. If given a chance, he would ask the genie of his life to erase all the problems from his life so that he wouldn't have to fight them.

He shouted, "Where are the keys?"

The poor guard vibrated with the high pitched voice. Fear had made Kushank's voice stronger. The guard immediately took out the keys from his pocket and handed them to Kushank. Kushank gave him a disgusted look and started walking towards the lab. Raghu followed him like a little puppy, but Kushank ordered sternly, "I can manage myself. Back to your duty."

Raghu got panicky. He took out his phone and called someone. Meanwhile, Kushank fiddled with the key and opened the lab. Nervousness had seeped in the atmosphere. Kushank's hands fumbled while he pushed the door. It was absolutely dark inside. Everything looked strange and this scared Kushank further. The lights were switched off, the lab was filled with an uncertain void and the silence added to the blank atmosphere. Kushank felt strange and fretful for a moment but then, he gathered his breath and switched on the lights.

As the lights were lit, Kushank saw the lab in a state of mess. Each passing second increased the rate at which his heart thudded. The broken test tubes and lab instruments lay on the floor. Some of the lights were broken as well. It seemed like a murder had taken place. Kushank was worried. The thought of 'what he would answer' was in itself very scary. The very thought that the media would scrutinize SVS until they ran it in their breaking news for an hour or so made him weak in the knees. Murder or attempt to murder in a medical college is sensational news and it would get them high TRPs, after all. However, the institute would fall from the top ranks into an uncertain darkness. Kushank could not afford that. He sweated profusely.

He didn't want to move ahead, he didn't want to face anything horrible, he didn't want to see what had happened, but he gathered the courage to face the worse. He made his way in between the tables of the lab and just when he was wondering what had happened, he found a bag kept near the small instrument room. The little bag was his only hope to understand what had happened, or with whom. But, while he bent to get hold of the bag, his eyes caught the temperature set for the instrument room.

It was set at minus sixteen degrees. He peeped inside the small room and saw something on the floor. The dimensions of the object suggested it was a human. Kushank panicked for a moment, but gathered his shattering self.

He immediately switched off the temperature and tried to get inside the locked doors. Meanwhile, as he looked closer, he shouted, "Hey, get up!"

It was definitely a human. It was a girl, lying inside – unconscious. Kushank tried to push through the vacuum doors, but he was doubtful of her survival. Which human could stay alive in minus sixteen degrees? However, he brushed all the negativity away and as soon as he unlocked the door, he rushed inside. He didn't waste time; he picked up the girl and briskly walked outside the small room, into the lab.

It is said, at times just one moment makes you fall prey to a feeling commonly known as love. The minute Kushank picked her up and started to walk towards the door, he saw amidst shaded light the face which he had certainly seen before. The girl's open hair touched his arms, her eyes looked serene and her petite body was as cold as ice. That moment, Kushank was distracted for sure. He knew the person whom he was carrying in his arms. They had met before. She had attracted him before.

But ignoring all his emotions, he quickly laid her back on the table and checked her nerves. The girl was fortunately alive. He let out a sigh of relief, but the next moment, he thought about the college's reputation. What if the media made a mountain of a molehill? What if the license was snatched by the association? What if the girl's family filed a case? What if he was jailed? What would Mrs Khanna say? What would happen to SVS?

He got nervous. Kushank knew that the girl had to be fine, else he would no longer be fine. He rubbed her back, her feet and covered her with the shirt he was wearing because the jumpsuit she wore hardly covered her.

She started to respond after minutes of warming her palms and feet. But, she was still unconscious. Kushank started feeling nervous. He didn't want to let any doctor see her because he knew gossip flew faster than light. Kushank was a dedicated leader. To save his college from negative publicity, he could risk her life. To protect her from gossips, he could afford to lose her.

The only good thing which he did at that moment was that he remained persistent. He didn't give up on her. He just kept rubbing her palms and feet. She was responding, though bleakly. He stayed patient and then, as she started to respond, Kushank thought about the condition of the lab. He started feeling scared. His heart broke thinking of the worst actions that could be taken against him or the college, but at present he kept his attention limited to the girl.

She had to be saved.

He deliberately shooed away all the negative thoughts; he knew he wasn't capable of handling such problems. Ignorance was an escape for him at that moment. *It always was.* All he prayed, wished, asked for was her survival. But when she stopped reacting to his continuous efforts, Kushank couldn't help but call his last resort.

Though he was hesitant, he called Dr Kashish, one of the gynaecologists at SVS. He had known her even before he came to Bhopal. They were good acquaintances. She answered the call in a sleepy voice as Kushank asked hastily, "Are you on duty, Kashish?"

The doctor replied, "Not at the moment. Is there an emergency, Kushank?"

"By when can you reach the college...earliest?" he asked, baffled.

"In ten minutes," she assured him.

"Alright, I am waiting for you in the biochemical lab. And don't tell anyone about anything. Be doubly sure nobody sees you come here."

It was exceptionally hard for Kushank to wait for the next ten minutes. The girl, whom he had met that day, amidst the rain with a football, had certainly left traces on his mind. It was miserable for him to look at her in such a helpless condition.

While he was gazing at the girl, he held her hand and kept rubbing it, thinking of his first encounter with her. Her current state was contradictory to the confidence that she carried that day. That feeling immediately made him hold her hands tighter. He was fearful of losing her, even without knowing who she was and what she was doing there. Perhaps, humanity. Or —

Meanwhile, Dr Kashish came running inside and checked Amaira. She said after examining her, "She's fine. You took her out in time. Just keep her warm with a quilt for a few hours, she'll regain consciousness."

A wave of calmness flowed through Kushank after hearing this. His college was safe, he was safe and even the girl was safe!

Kashish asked him as she sat beside him on the floor.

"How did all this happen?"

"I – I don't know. I don't know who she is, perhaps a student? And I am clueless about what I should do with her at this moment. The hostel isn't safe for her if it's a case of ragging and I...can't..." Kushank said doubtfully.

"My parents are not as cool as Mrs Khanna, else I would have helped you. I would suggest take her home if you don't want anyone else to know about all this," Kashish suggested, being a friend.

Reminded of a cliché bollywood movie, aren't you?

The suggestion worked for Kushank. He, with some help from Dr Kashish rushed towards his car and drove the girl home. At home, he was sure everything would be fine if he could manage to hide Amaira till the morning. His mum left home in the morning and she wouldn't know anything about the girl.

Though he genuinely wanted to save her, his first priority was to take her away from the campus because he didn't want the case to be the matter of debate and controversy for his college. *He thought about himself before anyone else*. Practical, eh?

He slyly entered the house and walked to his room, making sure his mother didn't get up. He couldn't face any unnecessary problems. He didn't want to.

Remember, Kushank was phobic to problems.

He carried the girl inside his room and placed her on the bed, covering her with a quilt and locking the door. Mrs Khanna wasn't awake, but Kushank was afraid the maids would see her in the morning. He pulled a bean bag and sat next to the bed, looking at the girl who was fast asleep, or perhaps drugged. He didn't want to see her silent; he wanted her to be the one she was when he first saw him. He wanted to care for her, but as thoughts of SVS struck him, he immediately took a back foot and turned away. Suddenly, she reminded him of the problems that SVS could face. She *was* the problem that SVS could face.

Nervousness always took over his emotions.

The nervous self inside Kushank was troubling him and shooting questions at him. He had to make sure that this girl didn't say anything in front of the media and didn't file a criminal case against the college, else complications would start stacking up for him and his chair. He wasn't sure of anything, but he imagined the possibilities. Soon, his eyelids closed and sleep gradually took him in its arms.

❖

Mornings, I had always heard, come with hope, a cheerful start and some rejuvenating sunshine. The day had also started in a similar way, except for the fact that instead of the rays of the sun, a splash of water woke him up. Replacing the tranquility was the crash of the glass on the white marble floor.

He woke up – shocked. It seemed as if an explosion had just taken place over his head. He looked, troubled, at the girl who stood in front of him and held his mobile phone, all set to be thrown on the floor. Kushank sympathetically looked at his mobile phone. From his previous experience, he knew the girl could do anything – anything.

He exclaimed, half shocked and half asleep, "What the – what are you doing?"

The girl outrageously started to shout, "What am I doing…"

Before anyone heard her voice, Kushank kept his palm over her mouth and whispered, "Shh. Keep your voice low." He was yet again troubled by her anger. What if she exposed his college? What if Mrs Khanna came to know about her?

The girl resisted aggressively, but Kushank didn't remove his hand and she angrily bit his palm to free herself. Thankfully, Mrs Khanna had already left for college. She was overtly punctual. Kushank knew only his driver would be around. So he called up the driver and sent him to bring some unneeded stuff from the market. Meanwhile, the outrageous girl threw the phone on the ground in resistance. Her eyes were fiery red by now. Part of it was the effect of the drug and the rest was her anger which boiled with every passing second. Kushank tried explaining, "Just listen to me…"

She threw her hands violently in the air which resulted in a sharp hit on his face. Kushank struggled, "Listen to me. I found you in the lab. I don't have any idea…"

Holding her was becoming tougher for Kushank as she defended with rage. He left her with a jerk as she shouted, "*You!* How dare you. Bloody idiotic cowards. Seniors. Don't give me that story that you saved me. *You tried to kill me!* And how dare you bring me to your bedroom? What did you think?"

She pushed him angrily.

Surely, she didn't know whom she was talking to. She thought he was just another senior. Kushank was taken aback. Firstly, he wasn't that convincing; secondly, this girl was too difficult for him to handle. He tried saying, " I – I am Kushank Khanna."

Impulsively, she replied, "So? Why the hell am I here?"

Her voice seemed decibels higher than the loudest voice on earth. She looked around and saw another glass paper weight and took it in her hand. But just before she threw it down, Kushank cried, "Please. One minute."

Was she a person who would listen? She threw it down. Kushank walked towards her angrily. He held her by the shoulders and said, "I am the trustee of SVS. Will you listen to me for a minute?"

A moment of chilled silence fell between both of them and a strange feeling forced the girl to listen to him. He wasn't convincing, nor was he honest, but there was some strange reason that she decided to listen to him for once.

He continued, "I found you in the lab. Do you remember anything?"

Lab? Found me? What was I doing there? I just remember the mess. Arjun.

Fragments of the past moments gathered in her brain, but the raw data was unable to provide any information. That enraged her even more. The harder she tried to remember things, the more frustrated she felt. She looked lost.

She said, still thinking hard to decipher the events of the previous day, "I – I was at the mess. And that's all I remember."

Kushank looked at her. Her angry forehead had marks of helplessness floating on it, her red eyes looked confused and her expressions forced Kushank to help her. He genuinely wanted to see her the way he had seen her for the first time.

He said calmly, "I am not a senior, so you can trust me for now. Can I ask for a favour?"

"Since you have helped me," she replied wryly.

Give and take was the logic, for sure.

"Just let me find out what had happened. I'll be back from the college in an hour. In the meantime, just stay here and be patient. Will you?"

"I will come along." That was the stubborn decision she had already made. But, she couldn't come along. How could Kushank take such a big risk? He resisted and tried convincing her for the next thirty-five minutes, after which, he drove to the college to find answers to innumerable questions that he had.

Bitter truth; even bitter circumstances

OBSESSION, REPRESSION OR WHATEVER IT WAS, IT COULDN'T have been justified. By now, Kushank did understand that this was a case of ragging. But, how could it happen was something that disturbed him. And *he thought he was managing things well.* The first reason for Kushank to get hold of what had happened was his college's reputation, his image and his chair.

The zeal to save the chair is greater than humanity at times.

Kushank walked towards the security room of SVS angrily, taking long steps. As he banged the door open, he saw Raghu, the same guard deleting a clipping from the CCTV footage. Kushank immediately got hold of him and shouted, *"What happened? Speak!"*

Have you ever wondered about the phrase 'position defines power'? Kushank was least confident, but strangely, power had made him stronger. (At least for now.)

The poor guard cursed himself for coming back to delete the evidence. He shuddered with fear as Kushank shouted again.

"Raghu, speak up. Else, I'll call the police and I'll make sure they beat you till you vomit the truth."

The thin and geeky fellow was left with no other option except narrating the story which didn't end in the way it was supposed to.

❖

9:45 p.m.
5 days earlier
Orientation Day, SVS, Bhopal

THE SUN HAD BEAUTIFULLY SET IN THE TRANQUILLITY OF THE Bhojtal Lake in Bhopal. The breeze was pleasantly cool and the city was calm and peaceful. Until the flight from Delhi landed and a young lady in her casual shorts and a tank top walked out of the airport. Her hair was left free as she always was, her eyes had just one brush of kohl which made them look darker and finer. She was gifted with such sharp features that there seemed no use of artifice. The dusky complexion just added to her persona.

The girl made her own style statement and walked with grace. She was Amaira – who else could have such a description, after all? She had arrived with five huge bags of clothes.

Shopaholic as well as a spendthrift she was. In fact, one of her friends always teased her saying that if Amaira bought more clothes, her parents would have to buy another house to accommodate them. Amaira landed and walked outside the airport with fresh hope. She took the cab and in the next ten minutes was in front of the huge gates of SVS. This time, Kavita aunty wasn't told about her arrival.

As she walked through the gates, the realization of accomplishing a dream brought a huge smile to her face. She clicked a few selfies to save the moment in the memory card of her life with the gates, bricks and a few with the guards of the college. The old guards looked puzzled and amused to see the girl so excited to enter SVS. Usually excitement was overtaken by nervousness.

Bhopal was a smaller place, people looked at her with alien eyes and in no time she had become the centre of attraction.

The word went around – 'a girl in hot denim pants has entered the college' – and being part of the misogynist thought process that our society is, the first goal was to hit on her. Poor boys, they didn't know what was inside this hot nutshell. One touch could burn them with the outrage that she had inside her. *The hotness was volatile.* Amaira was volcanic – if she erupted, nature together would have to calm her.

Fifteen days had passed with the flowing breeze – shopping and eating. College was supposed to start from the next day. And the hostel aspirants had to register themselves.

Air traffic at the Delhi airport had delayed her arrival by four long hours, delaying her entry into the hostel. She was late for her hostel admissions.

The first visit was simply a trailer.

And of course, it was the sophisticated side of Amaira that the college saw at that time. If sophisticated was really the word! However, she walked in confidently. She wasn't scared. She never was. Or at least never let it show.

So, the young lady walked in and to her utter surprise found the hostel to be a much better place than she had heard about. The walls stood firmly at their place, so what if they were old and trite; the warden was a human, so what if she was strict and expressionless. The co-hostel mates were students, so what if they were fearful and rude.

Amaira smiled at her sarcasm and walked in with the huge trolleys and a travel bag clinging to her shoulders. She entered the hostel and the warden looked at her in sheer shock. She wasn't used to seeing girls coming in shorts to a medical college. Poor Mrs Sinha was unknown to the repercussions of the post-Amaira effect. I personally pity her. She was to deal with an active volcano.

"Ma'am, I am Amaira Roy and these are my forms. Please direct me towards my room," Amaira asked politely.

Rich brats and their attitude.

This was exactly the first thought which occurred to Mrs Sinha – typical thought which wardens usually possess. She gave a few scowls while she judged Amaira, and tautly replied, "Aren't you too early? The hostel admissions closed at seven. It is past nine now. The college hasn't even started, but your attitude has."

Amaira wanted to give a sharp reply but her mum's words echoed in her ears. Preeti had repeated to her a hundred times to stay cool. Amaira gulped her anger and replied calmly. At least, she tried to. "Ma'am, my flight was scheduled to land at half past six but it got delayed by two hours. I am sorry."

The middle-aged lady replied arrogantly while gesturing at the corner, "Amaira Roy, this should be the first and the last time that I'll let you enter late. Go to room number 19. Right from that corner. Go!"

'Once I know the hostel building well, who will require the main gates, ma'am', Amaira thought and this brought a small grin on her face which she hid immediately and turned to walk towards her room.

"The mess closes at ten. You better run and eat. They are not as lenient as I am."

Every word that the strict warden said seemed like bullets to shoot Amaira.

What an ironic statement, Amaira thought and walked her way. Her DSLR camera hung to her long neck as always, and she was clicking pictures and selfies in different corners. After all it was her first day and memories need to be treasured. And of course, Amaira had to share every bit of her new journey with Kabir and her parents.

But, just when she was clicking a picture of the beautiful moon from the arch of the corridor, a smooth yet arrogant voice interrupted, "Who are you?"

Amaira immediately turned back to find a good looking girl who had a morose expression. Amaira couldn't help herself from commenting, "Why does everyone look so disgusted in this place? It's quite cool, isn't it?"

The girl's furious eyes suddenly looked fiercer. She retorted, "I am Rini, a third year student and your senior. I am also the hostel president…"

Amaira made a bored expression on hearing this introduction. She liked conversations short and crisp.

"Hi, I am Amaira. And that's alright. I got who you are. But, why are you telling this to me? Do you want votes or something? Cool, I'll vote for you. Now if you don't mind, please excuse me."

And Amaira made her way, but Rini stopped her by keeping her hand on Amaira's shoulders. She furiously snarled at the rebellious junior, "Listen girl. It's your first day so I am being patient. You better respect your seniors in college. Rule list is up on the boards. Read it and you better follow it. Do you get that? Next time we meet, just lower your eyes."

Amaira's patience was wearing out. Her smile was replaced by a seriously annoyed look. The preaching by Kabir and her parents had also started to be ineffective.

If a volcano is stopped from erupting, it becomes more dangerous.

There was a problem with Amaira – if she felt something was wrong, she made it a point to not keep quiet. She was constructed in such a manner that she couldn't kneel down in front of the wrong. However, her ways were a little too explosive. After all, till how long could you keep a pressure cooker silent? The pressure inside her brain had started to increase.

"Give me one reason why I should follow what you say Miss President," Amaira retorted.

"I am a senior."

"So?"

"You better respect me," Rini insisted.

Amaira shook her head in a dramatic despair and said, "Just because you are a year or two older to me, don't expect my respect. Do something awesome and I'll be the biggest fan of yours just as I am of Sachin. And as for the rules, babe, Amaira does what she feels is right. I don't care what your rules say, but if I feel what I am doing is not wrong, I'll not change."

Girls apparently have bigger egos and the senior girls were not used to let their ego flicker even a bit. They had always kept their juniors pressed under their thumb and were not used to such answers. Rini too, had been a leader of the gang that enjoyed ragging.

To her, Amaira was a mouse which had rebelled in her magnificent empire.

She warned Amaira with rage overflowing from her eyes, "I am warning you. We are your seniors and *we* are the rule makers and rulers. This is my empire…"

While Rini was still speaking, Amaira got engaged in clicking some photos of the lovely landscape which was visible from the corridors, deliberately ignoring Rini. This enraged Rini further. She lifted her hand to snatch the camera when Amaira tightly gripped her wrist.

Cat fight, eh? She couldn't tolerate any harm to her DSLR.

Rini cried in anger, "Ouch. You bloody girl. You are hurting me. And you can't take any pictures here without my permission."

Amaira grinned and replied with sheer rebellion in her eyes, "Why? My camera, my eyes, my hand and my money. Who the hell are you to stop me?"

"Your senior and the…"

Rini was interrupted, "And the majesty of college, the honourable president, right? You know what Rini, I still don't care. And I'll give you some advice. Stay away from me. I don't like to mix up with people who are dogs in the manger. Oh! With you, it should be a bitch in the manger, shouldn't it?"

And this time, Amaira didn't stop. She just moved inside her room and closed the door on Rini's face. Amaira entered her room and took a few deep breaths. It was exactly what her dad did when he was enraged. These initial moments were special to Amaira and she didn't want to ruin them because of an idiot. So she tried to regain her smile as she moved on.

Her smile returned when she looked around the room. Nevertheless, she knew this journey would have a lot of hurdles. Ragging is one of the most brutal aspects of college life. Unfortunately, studies have shown that every year many lives are sacrificed to the beast of ragging.

Nobody knows where the monster lives, but everybody is scared of it. It is strange, in a population where the youth is said to be the backbone of a country, we are afraid of one monster which is spineless, yet has lived for ages. Can't we fight one monster as meek and cowardly as ragging which is so scared that it doesn't even come out in the open? It always hides itself in the dark.

But Amaira also knew that she was strong enough to face morons like Rini and her gang. Delhi had taught her to handle all sorts of people. She quickly stuffed her belongings into her small sling bag and walked towards the mess. She had got some nuts and chips as back-up, but kept them for emergencies (when hostel food was genuinely 'awesome') and walked down the corridor to check out the mess.

❖

9: 55 p.m.
College Mess, SVS Medical College, Bhopal

WHEN AMAIRA REACHED THE COLLEGE MESS, SHE FOUND some girls and boys standing on the table and blabbering breathlessly. She moved on to the dining area and picked up a plate to serve herself. But, while she was walking, a rude voice stopped her.

"Go and sit there first. The seniors are talking."

'Argh! These respect-hungry monsters!' she exclaimed loudly in her mind and replied arrogantly, "As if I care?"

But, that wasn't it. As she moved closer, she found the seniors speaking, and – speaking as if they were being marked for their ragging sessions. The more you speak, the more respect points you earn, Amaira sarcastically commented to herself. 'These guys are too serious about rules. I didn't mug up so much even for my entrances.'

And the poor fucchas (first year students) kept staring at them with fear and anxiety. Amaira couldn't stop herself from laughing. She wasn't habitual of controlling her emotions.

She broke into peals of laughter.

It was loud enough to draw attention towards her. Everyone was so scared that even this seemed scary to them. Amaira's laughter was indeed scary. Poor people, they looked so petrified. They stared at Amaira blankly, as and she was expected to be apologetic for her behaviour. But the 'expected' was never her cup of tea. She replied, "Oops, Sorry! Did I disturb some very important class? Sorry sorry, you guys continue, till then I'll serve myself. I'll sit for some entertainment after that, I promise. Anyway, it's good, you know. I am in the habit of watching dramas after dinner at night. Today, I have some live drama. That's a cool replacement: Idiots for my idiot box."

Insane! This wasn't expected from a newbie, and Amaira, let's accept it, was being too daring or perhaps dramatic. Whatever it was, her seniors were highly offended by her conduct. Amaira was sure that she wouldn't be able to go scot free after this episode. And some of her batch-mates felt proud of her. They wanted to do exactly what she was doing, just that they were enmeshed in the web of fear.

Ignoring the looks on her seniors' faces, she lifted a plate and started to serve herself some food. It was clearly visible that she was a big foody, though her figure confused a lot of people. Apparently

Amaira never gave a damn about her figure and yet her genes didn't let her grow fat!

And while she was serving herself with a chilled out attitude, every person in the hall stared at her with an expression of shock.

Well, in the last decade, no one had dared to go against seniors. Even if they tried to rebel, they were brought down by the torturous ragging, but Amaira seemed carefree. One of her classmates, Rajbir, who was from the same school felt proud of her and wanted to stand by her side, but couldn't. He knew what would happen if he stood by her. Even she knew the consequences, but didn't want to think too much about them.

She was aware, yet wanted to be unaware.

It seemed as if she had never felt the word 'fear' in her life, or probably, she had won over it. She sat down comfortably on the table top, tore a piece of chapati and dipped it into the daal. She was just about to eat it when Rini, by now her arch rival, came up to her, and jerked Amaira's hands, which threw the food on the white marble floor. Amaira was offended. She absolutely hated food being wasted.

"Don't you act smart. We are your seniors. Accept our conditions, else I am warning you, in front of all your batch-mates, of the dire consequences. You better respect us."

Amaira didn't move an inch from the table top and coolly tore another piece of chapati and chewing calmly, replied, "Are you stalking me or what? I know I am too hot, but stop following me everywhere I go! Or just a minute… wait…"

She pretended to whisper, which was deliberately loud enough, "You have started to become an Amaira fan, is it?"

Rini frowned angrily. Amaira continued, "And just to bless you with some intellectual knowledge, you know respect is earned, you cannot enforce it. And if you behave well, I myself will be good to you. Till then, go and vomit these rules on the plate of those who are interested in your idiocies. I certainly am *not* interested."

Crap!

This was the reaction on most of the faces in the hall. However, Amaira's conduct was being admired by a few of them. Some in the audience didn't agree with the seniors, but they felt making a fuss was risky. *Amaira was born in the moment where risks and rebellion was being distributed in plenty, it seemed!*

But the show didn't end there for Amaira. Amaira further turned to the seniors, "And yaa, listen, you were blabbering about certain rules, right? Continue, I am not interested, but the audience sitting there might be intrigued. Go, and let me eat in peace. You have already disturbed me long enough. Ah! Look my chapati has already become cold!" she exclaimed.

And then Rini signalled to a friend of hers, who started speaking again.

"So, for girls, the fundas are:
1. No jeans, no skirts, no dresses except salwar kameezes with two pony tails drenched in oil.
2. You cannot and will not talk to boys without our permission.
3. You have to come to our rooms whenever we call you and also entertain us whenever we go into your rooms.
4. No texting with boyfriends or friends without our permission."

Most of the first years had awful expressions while they heard all this nonsense, but Amaira was amused. She couldn't believe it was all real. She laughed out loud and commented, "Oh my god, can I please ask you guys a question?"

She waited for a response but it was clear, no one would respond; everyone looked at her with blank expressions. Again. By then everyone was sure that either this girl was mad or was high. Rajbir signalled to her to let go of things, but she didn't. She continued, "I was just wondering whether you seniors have a life of your own?"

She dramatically walked towards them and continued, "An easy example, if every girl comes to you seeking permission to chat

with her boyfriend, then when will you entertain yours? Insane!"
She smirked.

The mess was filled with a dreadful silence. Nobody even let out
a breath. But Amaira continued after a deliberate break. Rini looked
furious. Her fist was tightened and her veins were clearly visible.
Looking at her baffled seniors, Amaira felt partially victorious.

"Oh don't tell me you guys don't have boyfriends and therefore,
for 'entertaining' yourself, you want juniors? I sympathize with you
poor ladies. Go get a life!"

And while she was laughing without fear, Rini's anger had
broken the shackles of her patience and she walked to the hostel
kitchen. Meanwhile, Amaira kept chewing her food. She was a
person who could finish the last bite from her plate before running
because of a fire. It was food which kept her going. It was food
that she thought about when she was with it, it was food that she
thought about when she was away from it. Food was her true love.

But, if she thought that Rini had left the room, she was wrong.

After five minutes, Rini walked back with a villainous grin
on her face, holding a glass of boiling hot water. She entered the
mess, asked the staff to get out and closed the door behind them.
Crisp notes kept them mum. This was their first step to squash the
rebellion. It had happened earlier as well. While Rini was executing
her vicious plan, Amaira kept eating. But with every bite that she
took, she gulped down her fear.

Fear is a natural, human phenomenon and Amaira after all,
wasn't an alien. She was also scared of what was going around her,
but she didn't let it show.

Her heart had started to beat violently against her chest. But
she didn't let a single wrinkle reach her forehead. She kept thinking
of a way out, but it was too late. Rini was hardly two steps
away from her and Amaira was scared. She was trying her best
to brainstorm ideas. This wasn't the first time she was in between
troubled grasslands, after all!

She waited till Rini walked with the glass. It was boiling hot and Rini held it with a cloth. Amaira's fear made her take a step back. But the moment Rini brought the glass nearer, Amaira used her left arm to jerk the hot water and it fell near Rini's friend, burning her foot. A few droplets fell on Rini's leg too. She shrieked in pain.

Amaira smirked and got up. She almost thought she had won a war. Rini looked at her friend and both of them started walking. They looked down and walked hurriedly, but Amaira stopped them. She didn't miss a single chance of inviting trouble.

"I am not here to train myself in self-defence, but if you dare try to hurt me again, I assure you that I will certainly not take it quietly. Watch out."

Saying so, Amaira left the mess without looking back. She was cunning and cunning was exactly what she needed to be in SVS!

You know, Amaira was not always right. She wasn't an ideal 'naïve and pretty' girl. She was human. She did make mistakes. She committed follies. But even if she was cunning and materialistic, she was wrong against the 'wrong', which made her 'right'. This is what I personally felt.

The fight was against ragging. I agree her ways were too explosive, but her motive wasn't wrong. Why to go along with the wrong when right is an option? Some people say that ragging brings discipline. How? By wearing salwar kameez and oiling hair, you get disciplined? Come on! School's over, so we better grow up. We should control ourselves and certainly not be controlled by the monster of ragging.

At the same time, it is not possible for any one person to stand and fight against a bane as bad as ragging, because the consequences can make you vulnerable. But if we can stand up against the management for increasing working hours of doctors or increasing the time period of the degree and win those fights, then why don't we stand against ragging, together? Don't forget, if one person stands alone, the person can fall, but if a whole batch stands up, even if you fall, there will be hands to pick you up.

Behind the scenes

7 a.m.
Girls' Hostel, SVS, Bhopal

THE ALARM IS AMONG THE MANY THINGS IN LIFE WHICH works against your will for your benefit. And just like most of us, Amaira couldn't get violent with her phone when it snoozed ten more times to wake her up right in the morning. She kept switching it off, but Kabir had set ten continuous alarms, knowing his sister very well. Amaira knew nobody else but only her brother could be so irritating. She finally got up after the ninth alarm and in a sleepy voice called Kabir.

"Morning Kabir. First day today. And I hate you for these irritating alarms."

Kabir smirked as he wore his shirt, while getting ready for college and replied, "If these were not set, Amu, you would have still hated me!"

Amaira quickly got up and after taking a shower she got dressed in one of her favourite short jumpsuit. She picked up her bag and left for class. Ironically, she was a late riser, but never liked being late. While she struggled to move ahead faster to reach on time, she saw the seniors stopping everyone near the boy's hostel and checking whether they were following the 'rules'. Amaira felt as though she was back in class one. She talked to herself, 'These stupid people will not let me reach on time. And being late – that's not done for the very first lecture. Mom says being on time is important.'

Amaira had this strange habit of talking to herself and seeking advice from her conscience. Somehow, it always worked for her. She walked parallel to the lines created by her seniors. Well-defined was never her cup of tea.

Whatever it was, it was a treat to watch!

As she walked past her batch-mates, they gained some courage to look up at her. Her looks competed with the hot temperature in Bhopal and the aroma of her perfume was pleasant as she walked past briskly. *Didn't I mention, Amaira was fond of perfumes and colognes!*

One of the seniors looked at her and tried to stop her, but she walked away. Moving a few steps away from the lines, she turned back and said, "I am in a bit of hurry, let's keep the drama for after dinner. This time doesn't really suit me. Hope you understand. I'll catch you later."

One thing was certainly clear – tranquility was never constant in Amaira's life. Every time, the tranquil atmosphere was disturbed by turbulence; every time that happened, Amaira came out stronger, except a few times when the turbulence perhaps made her a little cautious.

❖

Amaira made her way to the classroom. The fact that for twenty decades the classroom had been filled with students made it seem historical to Amaira. She knew many well-known surgeons and doctors had, back then, started their journey from a similar classroom. With the thought positively ringing in her head, she smiled and ignored the dampness on the right wall. She focused on the moment and captured it with her phone. While she took a seat on the very first bench, her classmates followed suit and in no time, the empty spaces was filled with faces from all around the country.

Amaira sincerely took out a notebook and her lucky pen and waited patiently for the professor to come and start the lecture on anatomy. She looked so studious that one would misjudge her for being sincere. Meanwhile, one of her classmates looked at her from a distance. Obviously, the batch was told to boycott her and therefore he couldn't speak to her, but all he thought was how similar this girl was to him. He thought, 'Even I didn't want to obey these morons. I envy you for the spirit you have.'

Amaira, unaware of the silent observer, looked keen on studying. Apparently, this was the first time her classmates saw her looking so disciplined. The sight was disappointing for some girls in the hostel who judged Amaira to be just one of those who were desperate to be in the limelight.

They discussed how they'd pass with flying colors when Amaira would be entangled in politics. For them, Amaira's interest in studies was quite a big setback.

For Amaira, it was all about *one* dream. Once that dream starts bugging you, the passion becomes your life. And Amaira was as it is a stubborn challenger. Once she thought of achieving something, she would leave no stone unturned to reach her goal. She would fight hard for her dream. Amaira sat straight, waiting for the professor who by then was three minutes late. She was fiddling with her pen when one of her flamboyant classmates sat next to her and lit a conversation, "Pretty confident, eh?"

Amaira replied tautly, "If by mistake you've forgotten, let me remind you, you are not supposed to talk to me. At least, according to those nasty human beings. Well, that is what I had heard last night while leaving."

The guy fumbled with words and introduced himself as Arjun. He said politely, "Look, just be careful. We might not be open, but almost everyone in the batch stands with you."

A lie. A sheer, simple, honest lie.

"What's the point? If you are with me, stand firm. We'll teach them a good lesson. If you can't, do not pretend," Amaira retorted. She was brutally frank.

"Look Amaira, nobody wants to be bullied or be ragged, right? But at times, strength comes at a price. Haven't you heard of the torture by seniors? Just because of your style, do you want one of us to be part of history?"

Amaira was about to reply when the professor arrived. The professor was a middle-aged South Indian lady who wore a decent cotton sari with a printed border. She taught brilliantly and her class was one of the best Amaira had ever attended. She had heard SVS had a good faculty and the first class proved the word of mouth for her. At a time when private medical schools were deprived of a good faculty, SVS was lucky to have some. Well, only 'some'.

However, after an introductory lecture on anatomy, when the teacher moved out, Amaira picked up her bag and started to walk out of the class. While she was moving out from the door, she crossed Vikrant, one of the rowdy seniors. He made a face and so did she in reply. Give her a disgusted look and Amaira would present a shop of worse emojis. Rajbir saw Amaira cross Vikrant and just to save her from a bitter argument, he pretended to innocently pass between them. He whispered to Amaira, "He's very dangerous. Be careful Amu."

Amaira ignored the advice. But Vikrant looked at her cunningly. He wasn't among those seniors who admired her hotness and swagger. He was a cruel guy. And the brain, my friend, is a tricky place.

If good ideas can strike it, bad ones can also influence the system of a man. Similar things were going on in Vikrant's mind. He had been dating Rini for ages. Rini had obviously cried about whatever Amaira did to her and showing off to be a loyal boyfriend, Vikrant had decided to play the game of revenge.

The plan was vicious and devilish but as I said, if your brain starts working in either good or bad ways, it has the power to do wonders. Vikrant had already thrown the net to trap Amaira. All he needed was the right timing.

❖

In the mess, as Amaira served herself and was about to eat her food, Arjun sat beside her, bringing his plate with him. Rajbir, along with one of his newly-made friend Trisha went to bring their plates when Arjun tried being overtly friendly. Amaira had an intuition that there was something fishy about the guy.

Arjun smiled at her politely, but Amaira broadened her eyes and said, "Listen up Arjun, I'm least interested in talking while eating. Plus, your flattery won't work on me. If you want something, say it right away. I get irritated by pretense."

Arjun reverted with a sugary smile. "Amaira, I just wanted to be friends with you."

He initiated a hand of friendship towards her, but Kabir's call distracted Amaira. She took the call and in the meanwhile, Arjun's task was accomplished. He smiled at her and said, "Alright, as you wish."

Amaira didn't think much about it and ate the food. She had always cursed Ramesh, their cook and the dishes he made, but as she ate the food in the hostel, she was thankful to the almighty to have given her a cook like Ramesh. In the meantime, her brain secreted thoughts about Arjun. She felt him his 'over-friendly' attitude was strange, but then, hunger sidelined everything going on in her mind. Rajbir got engaged with a few classmates and didn't notice what had happened.

My grandmother always said that an excess of everything is dangerous. This time, it was literally a Sword of Damocles which lay over her head.

Arjun kept Amaira distracted with words of flattery. When Amaira took Kabir's call, her food was adulterated. Amaira had her dinner and within minutes was feeling uncomfortable. Her head had started to swirl and she had started feeling unconscious.

Vikrant had executed his plan. Arjun was the puppet that helped him do so. Arjun had mixed a drug in Amaira's curry which made her unconscious within minutes. She had fallen prey to one of the most dangerously planned conspiracies. This plan was obviously made public. The whole point was to imbibe fear in the juniors. There was a bigger aspect – it was a clash of egos.

Rini proudly addressed the batch of students, "This girl thought she'll oppose us and would escape so easily. I feel sorry for her. She'll freeze in peace! And keep in mind…if anyone else tries to go against us, we'll put you in the same helpless condition. The call is yours."

While Rini shouted loudly to make the juniors fearful, Vikrant and his gang carried Amaira to the biochemical laboratory. They gave some money to the guard who was asked to leave the lab immediately. All this while, every student was forced to witness the plan being executed. The seniors had decided to set an example to ensure that everyone knew about it, it was made mandatory for everyone to be aware of what they were doing to the rebel. This was the same old theory of spreading terror. Rajbir was horrified. Amaira was his friend. But what could he do?

Hushed voices in the audience buzzed. "What are they planning?"

"I don't know. But it's better to stay out of it!"

"Right! I also think it was her fault. These big city girls…"

And such views kept churning in the minds of the students. They were mere spectators, as guilty as the culprits. During childhood, almost all the fairy tales or the books like *Nani Maa ki Kahaniyan* had a small moral. One of those tales taught me that unity makes the impossible possible. I wonder if anyone of those in the audience had ever read those tales.

Some did sympathize with Amaira, but were too scared to raise their voices. And a few of her batch-mates didn't care. They were fine with whatever happened, as long as it did not affect them. Nobody tried to rebel.

Inside the lab, the group could have done whatever they wanted. But, Vikrant didn't dare stoop to any shallow level as Rini was keeping an eye on him.

His plan was to directly kill the spirit of hope in SVS. He placed Amaira in the small room inside the lab where the temperature could be monitored and set. He laid Amaira there and set the temperature to minus sixteen degrees, after which he locked the lab, ensuring nobody could save her.

And once he executed his plan, he walked out like a tiger and shouted, "If you want to be free, be like Amaira. But, if you want to be alive, worship us. That girl is too hot. She needs to know what being cold is. Cold till she stops breathing."

In the audience was Arjun, who felt a wave of guilt flow through his spine, but at that moment, he was helpless. I wonder what made him such a coward. Couldn't he take a stand? He looked down in distress and thought about the first mistake he made. Perhaps he was simply a use and throw tissue paper for the seniors. Perhaps it was Vikrant's degrading beating which had forced him to be a part of this vicious plan. He was guilty, he was worried and he was tense. That was the bitter truth, but did that have the power to kill someone?

Trash should be thrown in the dustbin

Present
Kushank's Cabin
SVS Medical College, Bhopal

IN HIS TWENTY-SEVEN YEARS OF LIFE, KUSHANK HAD READ headlines about ragging and bullying, but the general belief in his mind was that the newspapers exaggerated the issue to create sensational headlines. Therefore, when he made changes in SVS, he didn't give much heed to the issue. And now, he was left gaping at his failure. His palms were sweating because of the stress. In the past one hour, he had faced many nervous attacks while hearing the story unveil. He was scared of losing her.

The mere thought that Amaira had gone through so much sent chills down his spine. The girl who was bubbly and unaffected by anything had gone through the darkest minutes of her life, he was sure. The very thought of 'If I didn't see her...' troubled him. He held the guard by his collar and asked him to leave immediately as he completed the story. Kushank shouted at him, "If I ever see you in my college, I'll not leave you. Get out!"

The fretful creature ran out of the cabin and left the college. Meanwhile, Kushank reclined on his chair and blamed himself for the fuss that had been created. Had he been stricter about the issue of ragging, he would have been able to save Amaira of all the pain that she was forced to go through. His brain began to process solutions to fix the problem.

He was sure about the fact that Amaira wouldn't stay mum and he didn't have the ability or power to suppress her voice. He had to think of a way to get out of the mess, else SVS would fall into the darkness of negative publicity.

With these thoughts hovering constantly in his mind, he picked up his mobile phone and got up to leave. Just then, Mr Kumar entered his cabin. Kushank asked, looking lost, "Yes Mr Kumar. Is it urgent? I have some important work."

Mr Kumar explained, "Yes, sir. I had spoken to you about the pay hike of the junior doctors. Did you think about it, sir?"

Kushank tried to come out of the shock which had just been narrated to him and tried to focus on Mr Kumar's words. He replied, disconnected, "I did and I don't think we need to increase the pay right away. Rather, we have been giving a lot of perks."

"But sir, they might plan a strike soon and we'd be in a fix if that happens."

"Strike?" Kushank questioned, pretending to be unaware of the word.

One by one, problems were making a web around him. He thought for a moment and then, stated, "That's my final decision. No pay hike for the next six months at least. We already have a huge amount of expenditure on our heads. Let them strike, we will hire another set of junior doctors."

"But sir, that's impossible. From where would we get them?"

"Come on, Mr Kumar. Employing is never impossible. If at all the junior doctors and their union plan a strike or anything, which attracts negative publicity, tell them to keep their resignations handy."

"But s-sir…that's unjust," Mr Kumar struggled.

"Nothing that keeps our reputation intact is unjust, sir."

He replied and left his cabin, leaving behind a confused Mr Kumar.

At that moment, any strike didn't strike Kushank's mind as all he could think of was Amaira. At the same time, he was an hour late. And keeping Amaira waiting would mean trouble. He drove as fast as he could. While inserting the key into the main door, he heard the sound of glass breaking. The glassware of the house was in trouble.

As he opened the door, he saw that Amaira had already broken a set of brand new glass bowls and had angrily picked up the glass photo frame. Kushank intervened and ran to stop her. He held her hands and took the photo frame. She shouted, "You said one hour! I hate waiting."

Kushank looked around. He was sure that she hated to wait. The floor was covered with pieces of glass, and his room was filled with paper. Amaira had taken out her aggression on the papers and glass. Kushank knew he would be in trouble when his mom returned in the evening. But, for a moment he focused on calming her down, "Relax. Okay, I know I am late. I am sorry."

Amaira was nowhere near being calm. She shrugged, less aggressively though, "Leave me. I have some important stuff to find out in college. That guy Arjun. I am sure he adulterated my food because he sat near me in the mess and…"

Her voice became low. She had tried desperately hard to regain her memory and remembering the broken fragments of memory were torturous for her. Kushank knew from her nature that she would investigate every detail. She wouldn't keep quiet. She was irrationally stubborn. And that was dangerous for his college. He said, "I'll tell you, Amaira."

He made her sit on the couch and narrated the whole story to her. Amaira looked ferocious. She said, "Now you wait and watch what I'll do to this Vikrant."

Kushank looked into her red eyes and saw immense anger. He *had to* convince her, else SVS would land into legal trouble. He said, "Can I ask you for something?"

"What?" was all that she said, perhaps plotting a plan to teach the seniors a lesson. She could be cunning and she believed in the policy of tit for tat.

"Could you please not call the cops and the media?" Kushank proposed.

"Give me one reason why I shouldn't?" she asked confidently.

Then, after a minute of silence she asked, "Or is it that you saved me because you wanted to suppress my voice? The owner of SVS would never want the media to cover this."

Kushank looked down. Aptly, part of the reason to save Amaira was his own interest, and the rest fifty percent was perhaps for the sake of humanity! Kushank's expressions made the scenario clear to Amaira. She thought for a moment and then declared, "Well, thank you for saving my life, but I didn't ask for it. And I am not going to acknowledge your generosity, Mr Khanna. I will call the cops and expose the ragging scene in SVS."

Kushank was losing the battle. He had to stop her. Even if he was under-confident, he had a sharp mind. Sharper than the confidence he possessed for sure. He had to play smarter. He replied, "Sure you can. Next month we have the inspection by the Medical Council and they are already sceptical towards private institutions. If at all they decline our license, you'll not get your degree. If that is fine with you, go ahead. Here, take my phone to call them."

For the first time during the entire conversation, Amaira found Kushank convincing. He knew this had to work. She looked thoughtful and realized her dreams were linked to her decision. She kept quiet and thought for as long as ten minutes, her eyes closed.

Kushank carefully observed her without saying anything. He had been successful, he was sure. This was the same way in which he convinced his clients and investors. Amaira thought of all the pros and cons and finally spoke, "But, I am not planning to be a silent sufferer."

"Who is asking you to be one? Look, I have a plan."

He smiled inside, knowing his words had worked. He continued, "I am not asking you to keep quiet, Amaira. I know you won't. I still remember the mail!" He grinned and narrated, "Listen, I have a plan which would serve as a perfect revenge for you, but wouldn't hurt the college's reputation. Two birds with one stone."

And Kushank narrated the whole plan to the girl sitting in front of him. In between, Amaira would interrupt unnecessarily and Kush would simply smile at her. She would fumble while calling him sir or Kushank. But as Kushank unfolded the plan, Amaira looked at him with excited eyes. Sure, it was an action-packed plan. That was the sole reason Amaira happily agreed to be his partner in crime.

Kush's plan was to portray the real as framed.

He suggested that Amaira agree on saying that her experience was all planned by the management and it was a step deliberately taken to keep a check on the ground level reality and loopholes in their administration.

Vikrant and Rini and the others would get their punishment, and SVS would be publicized for a new leader and novel ways.

Amaira agreed.

Anything apart from the conventional attracted her. In between, she suggested, "Why don't we play a ghost game with these seniors? Just imagine, sir! It would be so much gothic fun."

For a change, she looked happy. There was a bond that connected them, though the connections were, to be frank, materialistic.

Kushank smiled and replied, "Of course, the headlines would be: The Ghostly College of SVS."

Both of them laughed in unison. Kushank said, keeping all the problems aside for a moment, for the first time: "Go and freshen up, Amaira. Tie your hair, they are no less than ghost-like tresses."

She smiled and got up to leave, when all of a sudden she exclaimed, "Oh freak! Kabir! He'd kill me for not calling him. Can I have your phone, Kushank?"

Kushank looked a little baffled. Perhaps it was her boyfriend whom she wanted to call. He felt uneasy as he handed her the phone. Amaira dialled the number and had a tough time calming her questioning brother. She just ended saying, "Sorry Kabir. Stop lecturing now. I promise I'll not repeat this ever again. I was...just caught up with friends."

He retorted, "Friends? Since when have you started making friends so early? Shut the hell up and out with the truth, Amu."

Amaira made a vague excuse and disconnected the call. She didn't want Kabir to worry. She handed the phone back to Kushank. He couldn't stop himself from asking curiously, "Boyfriend?"

Amaira laughed. "What's that?"

Kushank looked embarrassed. He didn't want to ask this question, but at the same time, he wanted to know who it was. He struggled with words when Amaira laughed saying, "He's my brother. My best friend, to be precise."

This one sentence had given unknown happiness to Kushank. He didn't acknowledge it, but smiled. Amaira got up and walked towards the wash room, leaving behind Kushank, smiling to himself.

Amaira was one person being with whom Kushank forgot everything else. In just thirteen hours, her company had started to affect him. Her nature was just the opposite of his and probably, that was the reason Kushank had started to admire her even more. He was smitten by her over-confidence and the way in which she lived her life. Her carefree nature was contagious and Kushank started feeling rejuvenated in a way, until the thought of SVS came back to him. He knew there were a lot of hurdles in executing this lie. And the moment he thought about that lie, his nervous self was redeemed.

He immediately called Vishesh for technical support to break the news. Everything that becomes viral these days happens with an insane flow of money, after all. After listening to the whole story, Vishesh assured him, "Don't worry. I'll handle the technical aspect and we'll make sure SVS trends at the top numbers in social media. Be tension free from my end, Kush. We have done this for our apps too, it's not a big deal for us."

The drunk Vishesh had almost forgotten everything today. His alcohol had spoken the previous night. He was behaving normally.

That's why I say: even a drop of the beastly alcohol makes you vulnerable.

Kushank then called Mr Kumar and asked him to arrange for a press conference in two hours. Mr Kumar was confused. He thought that the kid had gone crazy.

Meanwhile, Kushank had sent the details to Vishesh. He made sure things looked natural, even when they weren't. He had in the meantime also called the editor of a local daily and given him the details.

"...Mittal ji, even you know how ragging is widespread in medical colleges. We just thought if our steps could help stop ragging in the colleges, then why not expose it. Kindness is a boon, sir. I'll share all the information with you. I am sure it will make a sensational headline for tomorrow."

It certainly was. Vishesh was also prepared with his team. He notified Kushank, "Kush, we are all set. But, we'll start once you are done with the press conference. I never knew you were such a good leader!"

Kushank looked down in embarrassment. He had not done anything which could make him proud, but the image which he intended to create was similar to what Vishesh thought. Amaira, who came tying her hair in a neat high pony tail saw Kush working hard for the publicity. She walked up to him and commented, "You are a smart player."

He felt she was taunting him. But at the moment, he could ignore everything for his college's reputation. His self-interest was his primary concern. He called his mother and shared the plan.

Mrs Khanna wasn't entirely convinced. She was doubtful, but if it was for the good, why would she be cynical. She blessed him and wished him luck. She was happy that at least Kush had taken some decisions confidently. Little did she know...

Quite easy to frame, Kushank and Amaira addressed the media and students mentioning everything as 'planned'. Kushank had requested Amaira to mention that whatever she did, however she was handled, was all part of a plan which exposed how seniors misbehaved with their juniors. Kushank ended the conference saying, "Well, the sole purpose of why we..." He looked at Amaira and continued. "...together exposed ragging was to make sure that nobody tries it again. The names are with us and we are rusticating the students involved. Thank you."

Smart. Kushank had played well amidst feelings and emotions. He had very safely protected SVS from any negative publicity it could get. On the contrary, it would give him a boost as the new and young face of the institution. Just as planned, Amaira said the exact things she had been practicing. In fact, the kind of person she was, she described the framed situation as most realistic. Kushank finally took a moment to relax after the press conference. However, continuous calls, texts, and mails kept him engaged. As expected, he had hit the bull's eye. The social media was talking of how the dynamics of Kushank and Amaira exposed their own college and the like.

It's true; *an entrepreneur can eat, live and smell business everywhere.*

However, one person who wasn't so happy with the developments was Kabir. He was annoyed with Amaira and the risks that she took so casually. He certainly didn't buy the story that Kushank had narrated. Kabir knew Amaira was in a terrible situation, and that was why she hadn't called him. He called her and gave her a sound scolding, a true big brother's scolding. And this time, Kabir sounded strict.

On the other hand, everyone in the hostel was talking about nothing else but Amaira. Rajbir was thankful that his friend was safe. Arjun was fearful knowing that facing the girl would be disastrous. Others knew that the story wasn't true, but were happy that at least the seniors would let them live in peace now. That night was serene. And most of the students slept a sleep devoid of any rules or boundaries.

Amaira too was happy. She realized that Kushank had manipulated her, but as the outcome was what she wanted, she didn't care much. She kept a low profile in the hostel and slept after reading a murder mystery. She reverted to a few texts from Rajbir and some more friends who saw her trending on social media.

And as the night fell darker, she slowly hid herself in sleep. It had been a terribly hectic day for her.

Meanwhile, Kushank was the hero even when he wasn't. Everyone saw him as the new generation entrepreneur. His work, his ideas and his strength was what everyone talked about. Somewhere, his heart didn't approve of it.

He knew he didn't deserve even a bit of what he was getting. He thought about Amaira, her thoughts came to him naturally and were inevitable. She, on the other hand, was happy being herself! And he, he was a coward who had cunningly covered the black truth with a pure white cloth. *Conscience, it is said is an internal mirror.* Kushank could see everything, which was anything else but right. Yet, little could he do! Caught up in between the complexities, he tried to sleep.

I like doing things differently

9: 10 a.m.
25 June 2015
Conference Room, SVS, Bhopal

"KUSHANK, BE PRACTICAL. THE PROPOSAL FOR LOAN FEES and loan payment is not feasible. We will land into losses. I explained this to you last time too, but your clock has frozen on that single point," said Arun.

Kushank was all ears initially, but when he saw his elder brother nagging him again and again, he simply said, "Arun, I really respect you and you know this. But as of now, just let me handle my responsibilities," he insisted.

"Oh yes. Responsibilities? And you think by being popular for one day you'll handle everything right? Let me tell you, Kush, what you are doing is called anarchy. The junior doctors also came to me to complain about you."

Saying so, Arun left the cabin banging the door. Kushank was habitual of such incomplete conversations with his elder brother, but there was something he didn't appreciate. He asked Mr Kumar to call the panel of doctors, including the junior doctors. Mr Kumar loyally did so. And when all the doctors were seated, Kush started with a smile.

"Thank you for being here, everyone. I assure you not more than five minutes of your precious time will be wasted. So, I heard that the junior doctors want a pay hike. Is the news true?"

He turned to the junior doctors who looked nervous. Not that Kushank had all of a sudden transformed. Even he was nervous, but he tried to mask his nervousness with confidence.

"Of course it was true," he continued. "Being ambitious about a job is not a crime. I too have always been ambitious. I also understand that with prices going up, we all crave for a better salary. Fair enough. But the problem I have is with your way. Instead of talking to me directly, you guys went and complained to Arun. I understand you must be having a better understanding with him, but unfortunately for you all, I am the one who takes the decision here. And I have decided not to increase any salary before the next session. With a very heavy heart, if you agree to work on the same pay, I'll not keep any grudges...but if you don't, I will not risk my patient's life for your salary. Leave the resignation on my desk otherwise."

Saying so, Kushank looked straight at the doctors and then continued, "Look, I know the fact that SVS cannot work without the best doctors, but it is high time we work together. I really appreciate Dr Kashish and Dr Gill who were the two people who had not joined the union. Look folks, I promise I will not exploit you, but you also need to understand that at the present moment, SVS is struggling through a few losses and a lot of expenditure. Bear with me. That's all. Have a good day!"

He moved out of the conference hall, not a person as he happened to be – confident and clear. He started to sign a few documents in his cabin when Vishesh called him and detailed him about the deteriorating condition of their business back in Delhi. They were losing clients. There was a sense of betrayal in his voice. He felt he had been ditched. This time, Vishesh wasn't drunk, and that made it all the more problematic. He did not shout at Kushank, neither did he talk sarcastically. All he said was, "We need to sort things. I would appreciate if you come back for a day or two."

The moment Kushank tried to step ahead, trying to be self-assertive, an invisible string would pull him back into the darkness of complex problems. And problems always brought nervousness in Kush. He went back to his isolation.

Kushank sat back and thought of how his well-built dream was slowly flowing out of his hands. He was confident in handling the marketing and publicity of his new and innovative apps; he was always intrigued by the new games which they created. But all of a sudden, he knew he was moving away from his self-created world of games and apps.

He knew thinking much wouldn't help. He had, in fact, always thought more than he could execute, and that was one of his crucial weaknesses. He didn't let his mind deviate from the files which were scattered on his desk and started signing the documents.

Meanwhile, Amaira was all set to leave for her class. She was wearing the same kind of clothes – pair of shorts and a crop top with open, wavy hair. It was the others who tried to change. The girls no longer had oil drenched pony tails and they looked casual and pretty; the boys could now open a button or two of their shirts to slyly show off their well-built physique, if they wanted to. The seniors had finally, though with great difficulty, restricted themselves from interfering in their juniors' lives. All in all, SVS seemed a better place.

As she walked towards her class, Trisha, one of her hostel mates waved at her. Amaira stopped as Trisha greeted her cheerfully, "Hey Amaira. How have you been?"

Amaira smiled and responded with the same warmth.

She could be normal at times, you know.

"I am great. How have you been? Aren't you from Delhi?"

"No, I am from Chandigarh. In fact, I have been missing my school, my friends, and the brilliant night life of my city. Here, there are no parties, nothing."

Amaira smirked as her new friend continued enthusiastically, "Thank God for Rajbir, you know, else that day I was in such a bad mess."

Trisha narrated how she had been accused of breaking the rules of the hostel by her seniors and was apparently the topic of discussion among them a day before. She had almost started weeping when her 'hero' Rajbir came to her rescue and handled the situation with much maturity. Amaira, smirking at the thought of a new couple asked, "Oh! That's really sweet of him Trisha. But, what had happened which was so dramatic?"

"Well, Rini had ordered us not to talk to anyone from the boy's hostel, but in the mess, when you were being targeted, they saw me and Rajbir talking. Trust me, we just shared a greeting and after that, we were walking back to our hostels talking about you – and that little thing blew up into a big issue. You wouldn't believe what Rini said that day; how shallow one can get. I had almost broken down, but Rajbir handled everything. He has become a really close friend."

Amaira heard the sugar-coated love story with a smile. At times, love stories intrigued her. And she knew that Rajbir was a good fellow. He had been an eye candy for her at school, after all. And Trisha was equally a style icon. Till a day earlier, she had been clad in suits which the seniors had ordered, but that day, she looked stylish in a pair of black skin fit denims with a yellow crop top. Trisha was about to say something else when Rajbir joined the girls, greeting both of them.

"Amu, every boy in the hostel is talking about you. Beware," he said.

Amaira laughed and commented playfully, "Let them talk. You know I don't care. But, yes, I do care about some fun. How does the idea of bunking the mess appeal to both of you?"

Trisha jumped with excitement as Rajbir said, "Not now. Let things settle for a while. We'll have fun. Don't worry."

Chatting away, they went inside the classroom. While Amaira was jotting down the notes in the terribly boring class, she saw her phone's light blinking, but just when she was about to check the text message, the bell rang. After that Amaira went to the mess for her meal. It was one of those days when the mess served food which was worth eating. In fact, there was dessert as well.

A few more classes, some little conversations here and there and a few formal greetings later, Amaira was done for the day. She made her way to her room when the warden, Sinha Ma'am stopped her and said, "Roop Tyagi is your room mate. She'll be coming in a fortnight."

Roommate? *And* Amaira thought she was lucky to have her kingdom independently large. How would the new roomie be? Amaira thought, but the next minute she knew she would make her good. Thinking about the changes in her room, she went inside and called Kabir. In just a while, the humidity of the surroundings ignited a feeling in her heart to get out and breathe in the open. *Trust me, hostels are the best way to test yourself emotionally, physically and mentally. If you sail through, it's nothing less than rafting through a turbulent ocean!*

As she moved out of her room, she saw some of her friends sitting and watching a funny TV series. She gave them a cool smile and went up to the terrace. She liked hanging out with groups, but that was only when she felt a need to do so. In the past one month at SVS, Amaira did gel with a lot of new people, but at times she wanted her own space – a rare possession to be found in hostels.

Most of her hostel mates were friendly and she always acknowledged that fact, however she found herself somewhat restrained from the usual world at times. That day was one such day. Perhaps it was nothing but hormones which were pacing up and down in her body. But was the situation really that simple? Were situations like these always as simple?

Anyway, Amaira made her way to the terrace which was an isolated place, but it seemed as if the love birds of the college had made it their second home. Amaira could see some dark bottles, some snack wrappers and other rubbish lying around. She walked to the edge and sat there with her legs surrendering to the force of gravity. She played the playlist of all her favourite ghazals and heard them peacefully.

It is strange, but even when a person is strong, at times there are moments of self-conflict. You tend to over think, thinking you'd find a solution, while the conclusions are harsher. You find yourself fixed in a mesh even more complex.

Our own thinking makes us go deeper and deeper into the complexities of life, and at the end, there is no concrete solution. Instead, you realize that there was no problem – until you started thinking.

Amaira was stuck in a similar situation when her phone buzzed twice. It was the messenger notification. Amaira tapped over it and saw a message which read, 'How are you?'

Amaira was puzzled thinking who could be thinking of her at midnight. It was strange. She replied, 'Who is this?'

She sent the text and waited.

'SVS's trustee.'

The message was accompanied by a wink smiley. Amaira smiled. She recalled the moments which she had spent in Kushank's vicinity. It had been a month they had first met, but it was just then that Amaira gave him a serious thought. The message made her think.

His mature and balanced thinking had impressed some part of Amaira, no doubt. He was probably the first friend-like creature she had found in Bhopal. But at the same time, she knew he was a very different person. She wanted to do two things at one time: first, to ignore every possible feeling which made her less 'Amaira-ish'; and second, she wanted some good company. Most certainly, humans need humans to be with at times; silence or technology doesn't always help.

Amaira replied, 'Sorry sir, but I didn't know you had saved numbers of all the students.'

She added a wink too.

Well my boy, if you haven't known the fact lately, learn. Trust me, it is a simple yet significant tip. Girls tend to send or say things demeaning themselves or portraying them as less important, but you better know that that's is the very moment you should uplift her position in your life. It is just a way to know the importance of the girl in your life and she at some point will definitely try this.

Amaira started feeling cheerful. She became happier as she chatted with Kushank. Soon, she switched from the ghazals to some peppy Indian numbers.

Kushank, on the other hand, always felt an urge to sit with Amaira and talk about his problems, confusions, dilemmas and nervousness, but he couldn't. He lacked the ability to express himself, but he felt she was someone who could help him. She was perhaps the friend he had always been looking for.

For Kushank, his mind was constantly distracted with 'the' moment which he had experienced when he first saw her.

That moment held a lot of power for him. Kushank also knew he had somewhere manipulated Amaira. She was probably a little too innocent to be fooled for the fame which SVS received. Somewhere down the line, he had demeaned her. However, one cannot live in guilt. Kushank found an alternative. He thought whatever he did wasn't solely for himself, it had been beneficial for her too.

Well, everyone had a different way to explain the tumultuous brain.

He replied, 'Well, not every student is as brave as you. And who knows I might need you sometime in life when you would come as a superhero and save me from goons or monsters!'

He added some laughing emojis. Amaira smiled and typed.

'Of course sir, and what would I get for saving you?'

Kushank simply sent two laughing emojis and their conversation ended abruptly. Perhaps doubts and the lack of surety had their own ways of playing with feelings. However, if there was something which this conversation did apart from confusing them and us, was to brighten the hopes for the two human beings who seemed to be greatly confused. Amaira felt lighter whereas Kushank felt younger – just as he was seven years ago when he started his business with Vishesh. Both of them had shared a conversation which was vague and ambiguous, but which had vibes of positivity.

Dilli

WHAT WOULD YOU CALL A CITY WITH EXPOSURE, RISK AND unlimited learning? I would prefer calling it Delhi. Yes, the capital of our country, which is in most ways one of the best cities to find the best in you. Be it gaining strength and confidence or gaining exposure, Delhi serves it all. Some of my friends narrated to me the endless nightlife of the city. Had I been a party animal, I would have enjoyed that too. But unfortunately for the clubs, I hate partying. For an author, a party means a quiet corner with a laptop and free time!

The metro, the highways and, what attracts me the most, the flyovers. The roads which have been designed in a curvy manner, the highways which take the load of millions; or should I say trillions of cars every day. The diversity, the culture and unforgettably, the people in full rage, ready to fight anytime with anyone. Apparently, Delhi is ranked as one of the most unsafe cities in the country, but at the same time, it is India's treasure. I still love *my* Dilli!

PS: Pardon the extreme temperature though.

And in the capital city of Delhi lies one of the most prestigious universities of the world – Delhi University. Without exaggerating, the university is no less than a miniature India – the same diversity, same politics and the same youth. But what differs is the thought process. At some point, you might feel you are a part of a larger country rather than being divided into smaller groups. That is the power of students.

And this eminent university worked on merit. The first cut off list had come out that day and the college, ranked number one by a magazine survey, was flooded with applicants. The cut off, however, shattered the hopes of many. Could you imagine the first cut off in Commerce to be 99.9%? The news channels highlighted and exaggerated the cut offs and covered a lot of stories around admissions, taking interviews of those who had made it through the first cut off list. The campus looked rejuvenated with a hundred new faces and a thousand new hopes.

The day was full of opportunities – not only for the students but also for the rickshaw pullers, stall owners and others. It was one of those days when they earned sufficiently well. Kabir got off the terribly crowded metro and made his way out with his bag hanging on his shoulder. As soon as he stepped out, the rickshaw pullers circled him and started shouting, "Mirinda College, twenty rupees. Sir...sir."

"SSRC, sir?" asked another.

"Art Faculty," shouted another. Kabir made his way and took a rickshaw asking him to go to SSRC. Being the vice president, he had to be there before time. The union was on their toes that day. Kabir strolled around helping a few juniors. He liked the ambience. Unlike Amaira's college, it was a happier place. Kabir was humble to people around him and looked at the lawns teeming with parents who had accompanied their kids. The new aspirants were confident. A few Delhi kids didn't take a break in showing off their 'Delhiitedness' as I termed it, but everyone somewhere had a little bit of nervousness as it was the beginning of a brand new journey. Something akin to the feeling you get when you sit on the driver's seat for the first time.

Meanwhile, Raghav and Anuriti accompanied Kabir with a few other union members to the union room. SSRC has a lot of money and their union room looked magnificent. Kabir sat back in his chair and looked out at the lawns. Some parents were stressed, some were very cool and calm. Some parents were arguing with the guards to let them accompany their children as their kids were nervous and young, whereas some of them were boosting up their children to go and complete all the formalities on their own.

Some students were confused which subject to opt for; some filled the very subject which matched their percentage. Some were clear, some were doubtful...but everyone knew this was just the beginning. A long journey preceded this embark.

Kabir was popular in his college for sure. Anyone who met him was impressed by his straight-forwardness and humility. Ah, not to forget, his diplomacy too. He was always politically correct!

He was dressed in a simple linen shirt and a pair of jeans. From the union room, he saw a couple of new faces and amidst them, a timid looking girl. She apparently had not matched the cut offs and looked disappointed. She was simple, in fact it was her simplicity which attracted his gaze towards her.

Disheartened, she turned to leave, perhaps to find another college along the campus.

The day was certainly hectic, and the warmth and humidity of the weather made it worse. Kabir just wrapped up his work at four and locked the union room, after which he started walking towards the Vishwavidyalaya metro station.

He loved driving and he undoubtedly owned his favourite sports car, but Delhi's traffic had taken away his love for driving. The journey from Gurgaon to college would have taken him five hours. The metro seemed a feasible option. As he walked briskly, Anuriti came running and pushed him a bit. She said, "Such a mean fellow you are. You didn't even call me before leaving."

As they moved out of the gates, Kabir retorted, "I thought you must have been busy with your lover boy."

Anuriti hit him playfully on the shoulder. She said, pretending to be angry, "Kabir, I swear I'll kill you if you tease me about Raghav. We are good friends."

"Of course darling, good friends who love each other are called 'good friends' only."

Anuriti frowned. She seemed cute trying to defend her relation with Raghav. Unintentionally Kabir had been the link over which they bonded. Kabir gave a smile which signaled 'he knew everything' and started to walk with Anuriti till a voice stopped them.

"Traitors! You left me with Sanaya and her friends. Do you know how much courage it needs to sit among them and listen to their nonsense?"

Raghav joined them, cribbing. Anuriti smirked and commented, "I thought you were very friendly with them, Raghav. You always talked to them with sugar syrup on your tongue, after all. I never knew they bored you."

Envy was evident in her voice. Kabir smirked again.

Raghav retorted as Kabir grinned slyly at them.

"Anu, I promise I'll never take you for coffee again in my life."

Turning towards Kabir, he continued, "Kabir, do you know what this idiot did? We both were sitting in the canteen and I just said that Sanaya looks hot. She just called her and asked her to join us. And then, this idiot got up herself, leaving me alone. I hate this girl."

Kabir smirked and commented in his peculiar style, "Oh! Is that the truth? I thought you…"

Anuriti interrupted panicking, "Shut up Kabir. Will you? And yes, the two of you, I have to buy some funky earrings today. You will have to wait for me."

Well, I hereby declare that the little shopkeepers who sit outside the metro station on the pavement sell the best earrings at astonishing prizes. The metal earrings were trendy and would go with western as well as formal dresses. Anuriti was just like the hundreds of girls studying in North Campus who were smitten by the trendy jewellery. However, it was as good as a punishment for the two boys to wait as they always did while Anu went from one stall to the other. The two sang in unison, "Noooo."

But, shopping is something which cannot and will not ever be affected by anything. Anuriti did stop and bought her pair of funky ear cuffs while Kabir and Raghav grabbed a serving of hot chilli potatoes from a nearby eatery. If given a chance, Kabir would eat everything and anything, but the lunch made at home.

In the metro, Kabir and Anuriti travelled together till the Huda City Centre while Raghav got down at the Saket station. The three were inseparable.

Touch wood.

Confession

27 July 2013
Yellow Line Metro
Delhi

"EXCUSE ME, PLEASE KEEP YOUR ELBOW AWAY."

The girl said timidly. Dressed in a simple cotton kurta, she looked petite. And it was after gathering a lot of courage that she had finally said this to the man whose elbow was constantly rubbing her shoulders. The touch was uncomfortable for her.

The man, instead of being apologetic, retorted, "Madam, if there are so many problems, then why don't you girls travel in the women's compartment only?"

The girl was taken aback. It had taken her three minutes to gather courage and object to that man and as soon as she did, she was bluntly refuted. The man's voice was enough to attract attention and the girl started feeling heavily burdened by the eyes which started to stare at her. Some co-passengers came forward to her rescue and started arguing with the man and soon, the conversation was not about the girl, but about feminism and patriarchy. In a minute, everyone forgot about the girl and started to crib about the 'patriarchal' society we have. Amidst this, Kabir, who was seated on the corner-most seat of the compartment heard conflicting voices and looked up. He plugged out his earphones and curiously asked the person beside him what the matter was.

He was a politician, after all. He needed to know what was going on around.

"Nothing, that girl had some problem."

He pointed at the timid girl, who was almost shaking with nervousness. Nobody bothered to calm her down in the ambitious debate about who was wrong. The girl stood in a corner, seeking for an escape out of the metro. Kabir saw her and recognized the same face which he had seen during the admissions. She had the same nervous expression even then. Kabir got up and walked up to the girl.

"Are you alright?"

The girl, who wanted to hide herself, nodded hesitantly, obviously not trusting the boy she had met a moment ago. Kabir looked at her face; it was spotlessly beautiful, except for the beads of sweat on her forehead. Kabir carefully looked at her eyes which made him take a step closer to her.

"Relax. Have some water."

He took out the Bisleri bottle that he had purchased while boarding the metro in the morning. The girl didn't accept it, but simply nodded again. She was sure she would cry if he talked to her further. Meanwhile, she saw that man get down at Kashmere Gate station and it was only then that she took a breath of relief. Kabir, who still stood by her, was pushed towards her by the wave of the crowd that entered the train. He took a step back, but was pushed two steps ahead. The girl certainly looked uncomfortable. She moved aside and her expressions narrated her discomfort. Kabir said hesitantly, "I – I am sorry. The crowd."

Wondering why Kabir was so formal with this new girl? It wasn't usual for him.

She nodded meekly. And in between the uncomfortable glances, the metro stopped at Vishwavidyalaya. The two of them got down as Kabir asked, "Which college?"

He had, very slightly, appeared as a 'gentleman' to her. His influential personality and decent looks helped her trust him. He didn't look like an indecent man. She replied hesitantly, "DRC."

Kabir made another gesture asking as they stood in the long queue to exit the metro station, "You walk till the college or you take a rickshaw?"

Kabir talked to her so lovingly that she, for once, wanted to pinch herself. It wasn't usual for her to receive so much attention. She was so simple that nobody usually took the pain to impress her. Neither was Kabir trying to impress her, he was just being himself, with a pinch of added decency though.

She took the bus or walked, but just for the day she said, "A rickshaw suits me."

Perhaps peer pressure, perhaps a sense to make an 'impression'. Kabir smiled as he said, "Come then, we could take the same rickshaw. That is more feasible."

She nodded again. Kabir found the girl coy and shy. In fact, it was the simplicity that intrigued him. He smiled as she left and he turned right for his college. As the rickshaw puller took the turn, Kabir felt a desire to turn back and look at her. He wasn't sure if he'd ever meet her again, but he wanted to meet her, he wanted to spend time with her, he wanted...

'Ah! Shut up Kabir,' he scolded himself and manually trained his mind to ignore such thoughts. *Ignorance, at times, is bliss. Or, at least we think so!*

❖

Meanwhile, Raghav and Anuriti had just come out after attending an introductory class. Third year not only adds to the age, but also to responsibilities, after all. As they came out, Anuriti smirked as Raghav looked irritated. He said playfully, "She would have thrown both of us out," he said looking at their teacher.

She retorted, "And you would have a problem coming out with me?"

He smiled back. Throughout the lecture, Anuriti had been pestering Raghav with different games on their notebook. He smiled thinking about his transition from the first to the last bench. He looked at her in a lost way as she talked, bringing him back into the world.

"Kabir! As always, you missed your first class. It was so much fun." She said sarcastically, looking at Raghav. Raghav looked away.

Kabir said with a notorious grin, "Don't tell me Anu, did you pr —"

Anuriti fumbled and retorted, "I have to take some notes. I'll see you guys later."

And she hastily walked away. Kabir looked at Raghav who watched Anuriti walk away. But he deliberately changed the topic and started fiddling with his mobile phone. Anuriti and Raghav were evidently attracted to each other, but confession required strength. And both of them tried hard to ignore the feelings – if at all there were any. Raghav and Anuriti both were commitment phobic, but Raghav, perhaps was more confused. For him, Anuriti was friend-zoned. He knew he couldn't spend a day without her, he knew she was essential for his life, but was it love that he had for her, he was unsure. It might just be friendship, why complicate things, he always believed.

She wasn't the dream girl for him, *if at all you allow me to use the cheesy phrase!*

I have always believed that there are phases. One phase might bring you closer than you can ever imagine and another might just tear the friendship apart. Time, oh time! Such a game changer, I tell you!

❖

However, later that day, when Raghav and Kabir were sitting inside the union room and discussing the budget of an upcoming event, Kabir asked Raghav bluntly, "Why don't you accept what you feel?"

"And what do I feel Kabir?" Raghav said as he looked up while working.

Kabir said firmly, "You know what I mean Raghav. Stop pretending."

"Stop beating around the bush, Kabir. Say what you have to. Else, let's just work on this damn budget."

Feelings confuse us. For Raghav, these hints, small coy moments, and teasing was becoming frustrating. And for Kabir, the dropping level of comfort between Anuriti and Raghav was becoming a matter of concern. Being a true friend, he had to solve it.

Kabir asked, frankly, "Why don't you tell her that you love her, man?"

Raghav didn't expect this. Kabir had never interfered the way he was interfering that day. He said firmly, "Let me work, Kabir."

Before he could turn to the president to ignore Kabir, Kabir stopped him and asked, "I asked you something, Ragh."

"And I don't feel I am answerable to you."

The atmosphere became serious altogether.

Kabir looked at him with a stern look and said convincingly, "Come on! What are you afraid of?"

He instantly shouted back, "Commitment. Do you understand this word, Kabir? And what's wrong in being best friends? All this relationship drama scares me. Just let me be. Anuriti is my friend – best friend. I don't love her. And even if I do, I don't know that."

And just when he said so, Anuriti entered the union room.

Dramatic, eh?

Accidentally overhearing a conversation can be disastrous. She didn't know what Raghav said before, she just heard the last bit that 'he didn't love her'. Enough for her to react.

She turned and walked away, disheartened and angry.

Having made assumptions, Anuriti was sure that Raghav had rejected her. But she didn't think whether she really liked him or not.

Feelings are real fools. At times, you can just laugh at the confusion it creates.

Was she sure about love between them? Was it love? Was he more than a friend in reality? She didn't think. All she knew was that Anuriti Thakur never heard a 'no'.

And no, it's not the typical obsession. Let's not really expect Anuriti to become the villain in this story as it often happens in melodramas.

Being the egoistic self that she was, she didn't wait to talk to Raghav. He, on the other hand, was terribly struck in between his emotions. He said as he saw Anuriti go back, "What happened to her now?"

Kabir retorted sternly, "Raghav, if you can't acknowledge your feelings, then just let go of them and at least make it clear. Do you get that?"

Saying so, Kabir picked up a file and left the union room. He called Anuriti and as expected, she didn't pick up the phone. She was hurt and in such a mood that he knew she would isolate herself from the world, cutting herself off from every form of social interaction. He was about to look for Anuriti when he got a call from Soham, the president of their union. He said, "Kabir, just go and meet Radhika. She is waiting near the metro station. She wanted to hold a two-day event in the college. Get those documents from her if you are free right now. Take my car if you want to."

Kabir quickly went and met Radhika, who was apparently interested in holding a two-day workshop to promote her post-graduation courses in SSRC. She had been pestering Soham for quite some time. Kabir met her and discussed the important details, after which hecame back to the college. In between, when he saw the gate of DRC, his heart skipped a beat quietly. Kabir was a social person. He was friendly with many girls. But this girl…Anyway, he diverted his attention and got back to the college.

Meanwhile, Raghav had gone looking for Anuriti. In the little time that he spent without her, he was drowning in guilt. She was a friend, a good friend and he had hurt her – perhaps knowingly. However, he still wasn't able to figure out whether he felt something for her apart from friendship.

This happens when friends around you are bent on making your life complicated. Kabir did that for him.

He looked around and finally found her sitting in one of the corner-most areas of the college lawns. He sat beside her saying nothing. She looked away in anger.

Ego was playing its game here.

He held her hands and said, "Anu, look at me once."

She didn't. All she thought was the fact that Raghav had rejected her feelings, even when she hadn't expressed them – no matter whether she felt so or not, but how dare Raghav reject her? Raghav then took her face in his hands and made it turn towards him saying, "Listen to me. For once." Raghav knew Anuriti was an inevitable part of his life and for the sake of their friendship, he took a decision hurriedly in his mind. She turned, but looked stern. He said, "I love you."

Anuriti looked at him and then said, "One should say what he means. Don't try saving our friendship, the relationship will not last long."

She got up to leave.

Typical Anuriti, Raghav thought.

She walked away. Without waiting for Kabir, she went home. Misunderstandings had cropped up in their relationship even before they were in one. Raghav too walked back with a dropping face. These were exactly the things he had always been scared of – the drama which came free with relationships. Even he didn't wait for Kabir and left.

Strangely, love as SRK says, is friendship, but unrequited love ruins friendships too.

He knew the explosion was loud and the effects might be louder. Both Raghav and Anuriti needed time to understand what it meant to acknowledge feelings because when unacknowledged, feelings start losing their spark. And ambiguity needs to be clarified. Watching a blurry image can, after all, get the head rolling.

And while Kabir stood in the queue to board the metro, he saw the girl he had met in the morning.

Sweet coincidence, he thought and smiled.

He didn't talk to her this time; he didn't have a reason to. She was with one of her friends and was smiling and talking timidly. She looked like a touch-me-not flower to him. He then got engrossed in surfing the net on his mobile phone. He thought he'd text his friends, but didn't. The situation demanded some space and that was what Kabir provided them with. These answers were to be found by them on their own.

Realism realistically

7:30 a.m.
28 July 2013
2/7, Kirti Nagar, West Delhi

MORNING – PERHAPS THE BEST PART OF THE DAY.

With every beam of sunlight, the button roses in my gallery smiled and blossomed; with every shine of the dew drops, my face always replied with a smile bright enough. And mornings for most of us are the most peaceful moments of the day, away from the tedious day ahead.

But in the Shrivastava household, the scenario was quite different. In place of the calm, there was chaos – shouting, blaming and cribbing about everything in this world. The head of the house by default was Mr Shrivastava, who was sipping his tea while reading the newspaper and shouting for breakfast. His wife ran from one end of the drawing room to another hurriedly.

The drawing room was small and cluttered. The walls were damp due to the water seepage from the terrace and the stains were covered with some picturesque posters.

Just like relations were covered with posters of pretence.

There were a few photographs which acted as murals next to the television. A photo where Mr and Mrs Shrivastava posed with their four children in the traditional dresses of the hills was visible from the corner. It must have been taken on a family vacation but looked old and forgotten.

Two of the three daughters were married and a son was in class ten. Their third daughter was ambitious and wanted to study further. She had recently taken admission in DRC.

She was the girl in the metro!

In the older pictures, she looked carefree, but now she seemed burdened. Perhaps time had changed the way life looked at her – or how she looked at life.

It's a two way relation, after all.

Across the drawing room was a little passage which was untidy and a right turn from the passage took you into the kitchen of their house from where Mrs Shrivastava shouted, "Suhani! Suhani!"

She screamed, calling her daughter. And in reply heard her son reply, "Mummy, she is doing her make-up. After all, she is the only person everyone will look at in college."

There were traces of sarcasm in his words. Suhani was perhaps the simplest girl in class; though her mother thought otherwise. She muttered while cutting the ladyfingers, "College! Since day one, she is just pestering everyone. I wonder when I will get some rest in this house."

Suhani, who had heard her mother scream for her, came running down the uneven staircase. She wore a simple blue top with a pair of jeans.

"Mummy, you called me?"

Mrs Shrivastava replied sternly, "Come on, help me with a few chores before you leave."

Suhani saw the time in her 'not-so smart phone'. It was already 7:50. She said, gathering courage, "I have my first class. I'll be late if I stay.

Mrs Shivastava said with a face as hard as stone, "Yes, right. To get ready, you have an hour, and when you are told to help, you are getting late. Suhani, do you ever feel bad for me? I just keep working all day long…"

The cribbing continued and Suhani, slowly kept her bag aside and helped her mother with a few chores. She knew it was just the morning tension of managing everything which made her so strict. Otherwise her mother perhaps was the only escape that she had in the house.

At least she consoled herself by thinking so!

She knew she would have to run later, but that would be better than leaving home with some bitter words. Over time, Suhani had become immune to such a start every day. Her brother, perhaps the only creature she literally had distanced herself from, said as he saw Suhani wash utensils, "Didi, I wonder how much you spend in one day?"

The kid was sixteen, but knew exactly when to touch the correct chord – when he knew his father would be listening. And as expected, their father started his own tales, "Chintu is so young, yet he understands the family's position. And you – every day you just spend so much money to go to college. Couldn't you have taken admission in the college near our house, Suhani?"

Chintu's grin made her more upset. She just turned, picked up her bag and left. She knew she was late and there was no point in running, but still did. She was earnest about her studies and that was the reason she didn't care much about what happened at home. She knew if she let it affect her, everyday would have to be a holiday because of some or the other reason. She walked faster and reached the metro station and changed the metro from Rajiv Chowk, running and struggling to make her way out of the crowd. Call it luck or coincidence, she saw Kabir once again. Both of them were latecomers – for obviously different reasons. *For Kabir, the degree wasn't that important; for Suhani, the degree was everything, but circumstances didn't agree with her dreams. Ironical.*

She immediately turned. She didn't have twenty bucks to waste for a rickshaw again. She turned but by then Kabir had seen her as it was a pretty empty train which terminated at Vishwavidyalaya. Kabir walked towards her. It was so unusual to see Kabir walk towards someone; it was always the other way round.

"Good morning."

So things happened exactly the way they were not supposed to for Suhani. She quickly kept her small phone inside. She didn't want him to know she didn't have a smart phone.

She looked troubled, not because she met him, but because she would have to spend twenty rupees for a rickshaw again. She had already heard enough from her father and so, didn't ask for any money. She just had seventy-five rupees in her purse, which she obviously couldn't afford to spend right in the morning. *And she knew he had enough to spend every day, why would he bother... but she had to*. She smiled meekly as he said, "Same time – again!"

She again smiled hesitantly. Kabir felt a little disconnected with her that morning. He didn't stretch the conversation much and started to look around without making her feel uncomfortable. Kabir had never known what savings were; he would never in the faintest of dreams realize her position. She thanked him for being ignorant towards her as she didn't want to be embarrassed in front of him. At the metro station too, she quickly moved out and started to walk, but yet again, Kabir caught up with her. He said smiling as he walked by her side, "Morning walks are always beneficial, aren't they?"

Since when had Kabir become fond of morning walks?

In fact, he was getting extremely late, yet for some reason best known to him, he chose to walk. He just walked steps closer to her, even when he didn't intend to. She smiled brightly, assuring herself that Kabir hadn't judged her for not taking a rickshaw. She was elated by the fact that even he was walking to his college. She felt accompanied. She replied, "Yes, I like walking."

Kabir smiled. He could feel the lost connection return. Perhaps, he understood. Perhaps, he didn't. He asked while walking, "Which course are you studying?"

"Economics Honours."

Kabir smiled and said, "Same as mine."

And just when he was to continue, Soham waved at him from his car.

"Come Kabir, I'll drop you."

Kabir didn't want to, but Soham insisted, "Come on, we have some issues to be discussed and I wouldn't mind giving your friend a lift too."

Kabir knew Suhani wouldn't accompany them, so he didn't insist. He cursed Soham for the wrong timing, though.

Kabir drove off with the college president, discussing issues and sharing ideas. Meanwhile, Suhani thought about her life. She knew it was tough, but she was sure she would pass. *Whatever the circumstances, just remember that you'll pass through them.*

Half the problems are resolved then and there!

She started her day again with a tender smile. She couldn't deny that she enjoyed his company. He was a stranger, yet she wasn't wary of him. There was indefinite warmth that she felt in his company. Strangely, she felt safer – perhaps more than what she felt at home. She just went along with the flow and felt there was hope.

That was important.

Midnight Sneakers

2 August 2013
Girl's Hostel, SVS, Bhopal

THE RIVER, IN ITS COURSE, RUNS ACROSS A LOT OF TERRAINS. Amaira's life was running through the terrain of happy lands at the moment. She had Rajbir and Trisha as good friends and she had managed to build a healthy relationship with her classmates.

She said she had friends.

But whenever she felt a wave of turbulence inside her, she wanted to be alone.

Anyhow, her friends might not be her confidants during moments of quietude, but they were certainly her fun mates. They went out at night to eat the delicacies of the small shops of Bhopal. Amaira was an ant. She loved sugar and anything sweet. *Mawabaati,* a desert, was one of her favourites. She could eat as many as she was served. In fact, the money which her parents would transfer would fall short because Amaira would spend almost seventy-five percent lavishly on tasty foods and giving away treats. Spendthrift was one word which was apt for her.

That night, the gang had sneaked out to have some fried junk outside the campus. However, it was always a tough task for

Amaira to move out of the hostel, especially since the warden hated her from the very first day and always kept an eye on her.

Amaira was not one who could be reined in. She always found newer ways to escape the warden. Rajbir and Trisha were inseparable whenever they sneaked out. Holding hands and exchanging sweet nothings, their chemistry was as strong as that of hydrogen and oxygen. They looked sweet together and Amaira was happy for them.

Rain had blissfully decorated the city. Just when they sneaked out of the hostel, the rain gods were generously kind to them. Truly a romantic date for the love birds – except the fact that Amaira, along with two others, accompanied them. Whenever they went out, it was a fact understood that Rajbir and Trisha would be in their own little world, isolated from their group.

It happens, folks!

Rain might have added a speed breaker to their plans, but it couldn't stop Amaira. She jumped out of her room window and joined her friends. Amaira was always a free bird; the more somebody tried to control her, the higher she flew.

The cool breeze brushed against their faces as they walked along the lake in the rain. Rajbir and Trisha shared a perfect story – a prince, a princess, and some love.

That's what I call a fairy tale love story!

As they saw the rain drops falling into the water while sitting on the edge of the lake, they could see the lights of Bhopal reflected in the water. It looked magical! In the drizzling rain, the city had a very calm and blissful atmosphere. Everything was just as Amaira liked – from the weather to the surroundings. She was elated and shared a lot of laughter with her friends and ate to her heart's content. *Eating was her favourite, right?*

However, as the clock started to speed up, Karan, her friend exclaimed, "It's 12:30! Let's go back. Amaira, come!"

She didn't want to. It was like going back into a cage. But the night was falling and if they were seen, her friends were sure that they would be in a real fix with a lot of drama. Amaira was with them, after all!

They took her, or I should say dragged her along and slyly entered their respective hostel rooms. However, Amaira had different ideas.

She never liked the usual.

Amaira stood near the window and called Roop, her loyal and loving roommate who was studying some chapters of human anatomy earnestly. Amaira whispered, "Don't shout or scream. Throw down my rope. Fast."

Roop got out the rope Amaira had kept under her bed, especially for such circumstances. Meanwhile, Amaira heard the guards talk. "Close the gate and go to sleep," one suggested to another.

"Are you mad? Kushank sir is still working. If he sees us sleeping, we'll lose our jobs. Go on the round."

Amaira was a champion in eavesdropping.

She almost started to like the workaholic trustee. She was fond of ambitious people and till that day, she had not thought of Kushank as ambitious. However, factually, Kushank was working day and night to complete all the formalities for the upcoming inspection. He had found many loopholes and while improvising, he was losing sleep.

Since Kushank had started working late at night, he had become a synonym for fear in the institute.

Probably, he had so much fear in his life that he thought, why not share some?

He had suspended three kids whom he had found drinking at night. Being young, he was lenient, but only to an extent. But alcohol was something he could never stand. He had frightened the poor kids by failing them in their internals.

Alcohol in one way, I see as the basic reason for the crimes in colleges. When one is not in one's senses, what can you expect from a body without a mind?

Kushank might have been an under-confident person, but he handled his responsibilities well.

I always say, he was intelligent.

He had just wound up some paper work and got up to leave when he saw the drizzle outside. Kushank was a caterpillar in a cocoon; he hated staying out in the open. He took a quick round of the hostels, as a part of his daily routine and while returning, he saw some couples sitting near the staircase. He smiled but was immediately reminded of Amaira.

Did the scene have a connection? Anyway, his personal matter. What do we have to do! Right? Or...

Roop, in the meantime, had thrown Amaira's rope down and Amaira was in the process of climbing up. In the totally drenched clothes and water dripping from her hair, it was obviously difficult for her to climb. Roop was holding the rope tightly to help her roommate climb her Everest when, she saw Kushank, who was standing below Amaira, looking amused. Amaira couldn't see him, but Roop could, and she continuously signaled Amaira to look down. Amaira, a little irritated, replied, "Shut up. I'll fall if I look down. You just hold the rope."

Roop, who looked fretful, in her nervousness lost her grip on the rope and Amaira lost her balance. She almost slipped and had closed her eyes expecting a few plasters the next day. Fortunately, Roop regained her strength and pulled Amaira up. The sincere roommate was always Amaira's last resort. But when Amaira started climbing again, a voice asked casually, "Practicing gymnastics, eh?"

Amaira got terribly startled and left the rope in panic. Falling prey to gravity, she fell down. Falling just next to Kushank, she forced him to fall too. Amaira exclaimed, "Crap!"

Kushank smirked. He asked, getting up and dusting his formal clothes, "You know what the time is?"

It was always in her company that he felt refreshed. Her kiddish ways appealed to him.

Amaira, drenched and shivering, replied, "Sorry sir. And..." She said pointing at his jacket, "...sorry for that too."

She made a cute, apologetic expression, like a kid who was caught red-handed. Kushank smirked and told Amaira strictly, "Amaira, this is unacceptable."

Roop watched everything from the window. A few guards saw Kushank and ran towards him. Amaira retorted sharply, "Weren't you a student? And I like spicy and sweet dishes, hostel..."

Kushank's strictness had gone away on a stroll when she began explaining so cutely. Amaira was innocently frank. For a moment, all his thoughts and worries disappeared. Amidst all the worry and stress, Amaira was a breath of fresh air.

However, returning to reality, he looked around and saw the guards and as always, 'what would people think' made him whisper to Amaira, "Shh, I am the trustee of this college and I have a reputation. Stop mixing that in mud."

Amaira retorted angrily, though in a hushed voice, "Then why were you scolding me?"

"When did I?" he said politely, trying to keep his image intact in front of the others.

Kushank was smitten by her attitude. He turned to the guards and shooed them away by saying, "Nothing at all. Back to your duty."

Roop, uninterested in the story ahead, left the scene and went back to her books, leaving the two recently-met old strangers alone. As they looked around in awkwardness, Amaira smiled formally at Kushank and he smiled back genuinely.

They walked a few steps towards the lawns in silence. Both of them were seeing each other after a long time. Kushank's heart already pumped 'special' feelings for the girl and that made him awkward. As for Amaira, she had just been caught red-handed. However, it didn't take much time for her to make a comeback. She said, as they walked, "I was really scared. I thought you'd expel me from the college. But, you're quite a sport, I must say."

Kushank smiled back and observed Amaira. Her smile attracted him the most. He replied, looking at his shoes while walking ahead, "You are drenched and must be feeling cold; come to my cabin – for coffee?"

Amaira replied, "Look at the weather and this lovely breeze, and you want to sit inside the four walls of your cabin? Are you pretending to be boring or are you actually this boring? Come with me."

Kushank looked at her questioningly.

"There's a brilliant tea stall just near the main gate. Come. And the lawns are a much better place to sit, sir."

She always added 'sir' as if she was compelled to. Kushank never liked it. Yet, protocol.

I wonder why a person like Amaira thought of following them?

Not the protocol, but the confusion in her brain – was it the trustee she was talking to or a friend? Perhaps she was too confused to find an answer.

Kushank replied, "Not the college lawns. We'll sit outside the campus."

Smart. He didn't want anyone to spot him and make a mountain of a molehill. Though Amaira wanted to question him, but for the sake of the lovely weather, she didn't light an argument.

As they walked, Amaira turned to look at him, carefully for the first time perhaps, and she saw confusion, tiredness and worry in his eyes. She wanted to know what was goin on in his mind, just being the intriguing self that she was.

They walked outside the twenty-two acre campus and sat next to a very small tea seller. He had almost slept after closing his shop. But, when he saw Amaira, he got up and was happy to serve her. In the past one month, there had been many days when Amaira would come and have tea there. She would talk to the vendor about his life, about his wife and at times would help his son with math problems.

Truly intriguing she was!

Kushank looked at her and thought of how different the girl was from what she appeared. She was a new person inside. However, when they sat on the small bench, their shoulders brushing against one another, Kushank could feel her touch, whereas Amaira didn't even realize it. She said, "Sir, should I appreciate you for something?"

Kushank asked teasing her, "For not expelling you?" He felt rejuvenated when with her.

She laughed a bit, then continued, "For being strict with the alcohol issue. I was proud of you."

Kushank hesitantly smiled and replied, "Thanks."

He looked lost, noticing which, Amaira asked inquisitively, "One minute, you look perturbed and confused. What's the matter?"

Kushank came out of his blues and replied faintly, "N – no."

Amaira retorted, "You are lying."

"I am not," he pleaded.

"You are," she insisted.

"How can you be so sure? You hardly know me," Kushank said.

Amaira dominatingly replied, "Will you shut up and tell me what's bothering you?"

The next moment she realized she was talking to the owner of SVS. But, somewhere down the line, friendship had started to blossom between the two over tea. Even Kushank liked the fact that he was addressed as a friend and not as 'sir'. The 'sir' added miles of distance between them, he thought. He looked at her and sighed. "You are so very stubborn."

"That I am. Is it some girlfriend problem?"

Amaira mistook Kushank to be a womanizer. The image in her brain of him was that of a charming flirt.

Well, Bollywood movies described most young bosses who were rich as flirtatious. Ah! Some of them certainly were. And Bollywood certainly had an impact on this girl!

She was wrong. His looks never gifted him a good relationship. He was too caught up to make a move. He retorted, "Will you talk about something which makes sense, Amaira?"

Amaira dramatically replied, "Only on one condition – out with what is troubling you. Fast."

At 1:35 a.m., sitting drenched and feeling the cold breeze, the two were enjoying each other's company. For once, they looked like friends. *But friendship?*

Anyway, Kushank finally, after repeated insistence from his fellow companion, spoke up, "I am in between two boats. My self-created start-up and this hospital. From the very beginning, I was apprehensive whether I'll be happy working as the head of such a big institution. I have a small apps and games creation business in Delhi which I started with one of my friends, and today, it's doing well in the sector. We are earning well from it.

"Now, either I choose my own self-interest over my mom's expectations or I compromise with what is best for me. I am an entrepreneur, Amaira. I don't relate with medical science well. It's not exactly what I expect from my life. But, Maa matters to me more than anything. It's just getting complicated in my head. Everything is getting messed up. Vishesh is slowly losing the trust he had in me, and I – I just don't know…"

Expressions were never his cup of tea until he had a cup of tea with Amaira.

Amaira heard him patiently, without being judgmental. She could see the under-confident Kushank who wasn't able to take a stand. He was confused and weak. However, his image in her head had almost taken a 360 degree turn. From the image of a rich guy who was enjoying his hereditary wealth to a self-made man, there was a transformation in her head.

She thought about it for a moment and spoke up a little playfully, trying to make the atmosphere light, "You are a complete package. I never knew you owned a business."

He smiled at the innocent effort. Then, Amaira continued, a bit seriously, "On a serious note, why don't you manage both?"

"Impossible. It's not possible," Kushank bluntly cut her.

She insisted, being the true Amaira, "Nothing is impossible until you accept it to be impossible. Have you really, I mean *really* tried?"

Kushank became thoughtful for a minute and replied, "Perhaps...no. You know, I had already accepted the fact that I cannot manage two responsibilities together. I did try and handle some work simultaneously, but somewhere, I had already accepted that things won't work out, so they didn't."

Amaira exclaimed, tapping her palm on his head, "I just don't believe this. Such intelligence and dumbness in the same mind."

Unimaginably true.

Kushank looked down pensively at her and asked, as if starving for an assurance. "Amaira, you're sure I'll be able to manage both my priorities?"

Amaira kept her warm palm on his and assured him, the way she assured all her friends when they felt weak about their dreams, "If you put in all the energy, hard work and zeal that you have and be positive throughout, I am sure *it's possible*."

One touch had made the blood inside his body flow faster. His heart too assured him that he would manage everything successfully. The touch was doing the work for him, whereas she was doing what she'd do for any of her friends. Amaira was a good friend; she was always there when people needed her.

Amaira added, "Kush, as a friend, if I am one, I would suggest you to keep going, because there is nothing worse in this world than to stop. Simply keep flying."

He looked up at her eyes. He could see confidence for him in her bright eyes. Whenever she motivated someone, Amaira became adamantly confident about that person. He could feel her hand being the force which was working for him. Amaira added, "I trust your potential. So, before giving up, try to manage both. If not for anything else, for yourself and working in the tech-sector itself. How could you underestimate the power of technology? Think of ways to stay be connected even while staying here. Work double as of now, and soon, everything will be perfect. Why do you get scared of working harder? This is the time, after all."

At times, if you find confidence for yourself in another person's eyes, you are doubly sure about your strength. And Amaira was right; giving up was worse. Just then, Kushank called Vishesh who was fast asleep. He called thrice; Amaira pushed him to do so.

Poor Kush was in a risky situation at the moment. Amaira's influence was dangerous for him. She was making him do things which she always did. If there's something good about to happen, why wait for the next moment, is what she believed in. Vishesh picked up the phone after six continuous calls. He first started with some abuses, "What the hell, Kush?"

Kushank said confidently, "I wanted to promise you something."

Vishesh asked in his uninterested, sleepy voice, "Couldn't it wait till the morning?"

Kush said in his charming voice, "Good times need not wait for time, Vish. And the promise is to stay firm in the business I started with the highest hopes. I am not leaving our world. We need to be the best first. I promise, I'll solve everything with you."

Vishesh, who was slowly losing hope in Kushank, could sense a confidence in him which he had never felt before. He smiled and was completely awake by that time. He had found the hope of standing firm in his business again. He said, "You mean you are coming back?"

"No."

"Then, was this a stupid joke, Kush?" he asked baffled.

Kushank explained, "No, it is not. I will continue our cyber world through the cyber world. When our business can reach the world without our physical presence, then why can't I? Trust me, together, it's possible."

"Well done my sher!" Amaira exclaimed in her mind. Kushank disconnected the call and turned to Amaira, "You are a genius." Kushank felt confident about himself; rejuvenated was the word. He could go home with a firmer faith in his dreams. He was feeling this happy after a very long time.

Amaira reverted, "That I know. Anything new to share?"

Kushank looked at her in astonishment. She was an alien. This girl had the same energy level from dusk to dawn. He smiled and commented, "Well, nothing new, but the fact that it's 2 a.m. and we are sitting right in front of your hostel and my office. Also, you are drenched. How will you go back?"

Amaira looked at her cellphone and dramatically repeated, "How-will-I-go-back?"

And she laughed aloud. Kushank looked puzzled and asked, "Should I talk to the warden?"

Amaira panicked, "Obviously not. I'll manage my way out. You can leave. Good night."

Kushank was stubborn, "I am not planning to leave until you reach your room."

Amaira insisted, "Not at all. I won't share my secret passages with you."

"Why not?"

"Because, all in all, you are the head of the college. You might dismiss me someday!"

But Kushank didn't relent. Gosh! A stubborn friendship these guys shared. Amaira finally agreed, making him promise to keep his mouth shut about her ways. He surrendered to all her demands. She slyly jumped over the back wall of the hostel and climbed the stairs for the terrace and made her way to her room. I wonder what the girl wore – certainly not ordinary shoes, they were Midnight Sneakers!

Hot boys; hot weather

5 August 2013
12 p.m.
Physiology Lab, SVS, Bhopal

SO BOYS, WHAT IF YOU WERE TOLD TO TAKE OFF YOUR SHIRT and lie in front of eight girls on a table?

Baffled-Puzzled-Embarrassed-Shy.

Wouldn't these be some emotions you'd go through?

Well, these were exactly what the poor boys of SVS went through. Shekhar Singh Raghuvanshi was one of the strictest teachers in college, who had in the past thrown students out for their 'misbehaviour'. He was one of the most successful doctors of the hospital, but at the same time, was the symbol of conventionality as a teacher. 'Protocol', 'rules', 'discipline' and words like these were the basis of his education and he wanted to impart the same to his students too.

He didn't tolerate any nonsense in his practical classes and knowing this fact, all the boys didn't say a single word and went shirtless without a second thought.

Official stripping, eh?

Imagine, all the twenty boys taking off their shirts and the girls simply checking them out.

Amaira stood near one of the tables and waited for the boy to lie down so that she could be done with her practicals. She didn't care much about bare-chested boys, however, even she didn't miss the chance to glance at some of the well-toned muscles. Well, you see it is a kind of attraction which magnetizes and attracts, umm – alright! Let's just cut the crap.

Most of the girls looked shy and embarrassed to see their classmates in such a state. Some of the boys possessed hairy chests, some had perfectly toned bodies and some looked plain boring. Rajbir was one of the most checked out persons and it certainly didn't go very well with his girlfriend.

Well, in that lab, the atmosphere was certainly not like any ordinary practical; it seemed more like a confrontation. The boys were very hesitant, but they lay straight on their backs on the allotted tables. Amaira, with a few other students, stood near the corner table and waited patiently for the allotted patient. She didn't care much about any boy with or without a shirt; all she cared about were her marks.

The lab assistant came running and warned everyone, "Sirji is on his way. Be at your places or he'll throw you out."

Everyone rushed to their places fretfully. Arjun ran to his.

Call it coincidence or bad luck, he had been allotted the same table by which Amaira stood. The flamboyant lad lay straight without saying anything to Amaira, because the Professor had arrived. He couldn't look at Amaira, for he was drowned in guilt.

That day after the whole ragging episode, Amaira had particularly named people who had been involved in ragging, but had excused Arjun, even though she knew he was the main culprit.

He could have warned her, but he hadn't. She could have ruined him, but she didn't.

Arjun felt terribly guilty.

Amaira stood still as she saw Raghuvanshi sir enter. He was a man in his early sixties and wore a coat even in the humid temperature of August in Bhopal. Protocol. He walked past the students and stood firmly. He guided the students with a few procedures and asked the lab assistants to help.

The patient, who lay on the table, had to be treated and the girls had to press hard on the chest of their subjects. Basically, the practical was to confirm that no doctor ever thought of any class, caste, gender or friendship when he treated a patient. It was indeed a good way of starting. The girls started taking their readings and when Amaira was done with the practice, Arjun politely whispered, risking his existence in front of the fearful professor.

"Amai-ra, I..."

Amaira turned away deliberately and started to leave when Mr Raghuvanshi's eyes caught her denim shorts and a tank top. He walked up to her and snarled, "What kind of a dress is this?"

Amaira was taken aback. She was the first one to complete the practice perfectly and rather than appreciating her for her work, he was questioning her clothes.

"Excuse me, sir?"

Whenever someone tried to teach her how to live her life, she gave back much in return. Knowing his nature, she managed to gulp down her anger, for once. The professor, however, kept inviting trouble, "No no, come in a one piece tomorrow. After all, we all are here to party, forget the patients. What do we have to do with them?"

Amaira replied politely, "I am sorry sir, but how does a dress affect my patient? My attention is on my patient..."

The lab assistant prompted Amaira to keep quiet, but she ignored him. She never understood that some teachers have an ego and at times, if you let them glorify their ego, they automatically calm down. Anyway, the harm was already done. Amaira had started to argue which didn't go very well with the Professor. He shouted, "Get out!"

All the forty pairs of eyes were now aimed at Amaira. By now, whenever something unusual took place, it had undoubtedly something to do with Amaira.

"There are rules. Protocol has to be followed. You cannot enter an operation theatre in a mini skirt," the Professor continued yelling.

Amaira was now being stung by the comments. She knew she wasn't wrong. There was no question of surrendering therefore.

She argued further, even when all her friends signaled her to keep quiet and simply walk out.

"Sir, for a moment please bear with me and analyze a situation. There has been an accident on the road, the patient is in desperate need of a doctor and I am supposedly in a party. Now when I run to the hospital, will I leave the patient in the Emergency and ask the nurse for my salwar kameez? Does a piece of cloth compete with a patient's life? I'd think of nothing but saving a life instead."

The class heard her in pin drop silence. Even when she made sense, it was just too unconventional for Raghuvanshi sir to digest. He shouted again, "Get out I said!"

The lab assistant walked to Amaira and asked her to leave. He had seen students beg in front of Raghuvanshi sir for marks just because at one point of time they had had a vague argument with him. Amaira didn't leave before saying, "Sir, I have heard you are the best teacher in SVS and also the best doctor who hasn't kept anything above his patients, then why follow these so called rules or conventions? At last, I am sorry for the misbehaviour if I was found guilty, but I will not change myself for the rules."

And she picked up her bag and left the lab without looking back. She walked till the lawns near the admin office and found a shady place to sit. She sat down under a tree as the netted rays of the sun made their way to reach her.

She thought about the argument she had had with the strictest teacher in SVS. She knew her degree was at risk if this fellow stood firm on failing her. Meanwhile, she received Kabir's call. He asked grasping her mood from her voice, "Is everything okay, Amu?"

Amaira explained the whole story to him, feeling lighter, "... you know Kabir, I keep trying to be calm, but everyday something or the other brings me to the centre stage. I don't want to get into arguments, but then, how could I accept my fault when I wasn't at fault?"

Kabir replied, "That's fine, Amu. Don't think much. If you think you are right, be firm. And be yourself – be it anywhere. Just don't worry. I am there with you, little one!"

That's how siblings are: always at extreme ends, but always there for each other.

Amaira smiled and kept the phone as she saw a few seniors walk towards her. She could see one of Rini's old friends. The girl walked to her and sat near her, making a conversation, "Hi Amaira. Checked out the BLT list?"

Amaira tried being polite, though she wasn't in a normal state of mind.

"What is that?" she asked ignorantly.

"Beauty List Topper. Come on, don't tell me you didn't know about this."

Of course Amaira didn't. She asked, amused, "There seriously exists such a list in college?"

"Yes Amaira. The rule is that girls make a Handsome List and the boys rank girls on beauty and I guess you are at the top of the BLT. You were unaware?"

Amaira's serious mood all of a sudden took a U turn and she was back to herself. She asked, "Oh, I see. By the way, can I just ask you a question?"

The senior nodded. Amaira continued sarcastically, "School's over, right? Then why aren't we growing up in college? I mean, what's there in beauty? It's here today, will not be tomorrow. What is the big deal?"

The girl sighed at Amaira's attitude and left the conversation midway. But one person who had overheard the conversation walked to Amaira and asked, "At times I wonder whether you are really mature or you just pretend to be so."

It was Kushank. Amaira asked startled by his presence, "And I wonder from where you pop up every time I sit thoughtfully."

Kushank smiled as he replied, "Well, was just entering the office for some work and heard you speak in the highest volumes. Anyway, why are you here? No classes today?"

Amaira looked down and smiled sheepishly. Kushank guessed surprisingly, "Don't tell me Amaira, you were thrown out of the class?"

Amaira narrated the whole scene, "...So, Raghuvanshi sir didn't like my dress apparently! But sir, he is a very very good teacher, I must confess."

Kushank heard the long tale and commented, "Amaira, I am really worried about my college with you in it. And listen, enjoy some nasty things too, you'll miss them later."

She retorted, "Are you hinting towards the Beauty Topper List?"

Kushank smirked. Amaira spoke with dramatic anger, "It's too kiddish."

'Whatever it might seem like, the list is topped by the most deserving girl in college,' he thought.

Amaira continued, "Sir, can I ask you something?"

"Of course," he replied.

"Am I being too difficult as a first year student? Am I too rude or arrogant or perhaps..."

Kushank replied even without letting her complete, "Amaira Roy, you are yourself. No need to change. People might not like you, but you don't have to care about them. *Some may even pull you down, but it is because you are too high for them to match your standards.* Phases come and go, but what stays with you is *yourself,* so never doubt that. Plus, I confess you are what I couldn't be. So, don't think of being like me. It gets difficult later."

Amaira smiled looking at the admiration with which her friend convinced her. For Kushank, Amaira had started to become a dream, a fantasy, an imagination...but he was too scared, as always, to accept what she meant to him.

Every relationship comes at a cost

4 p.m.
4 September 2013
Yamuna Bank, Delhi

LOVE WAS FLOATING AND BUBBLING IN THE AIR IN DELHI.
Howsoever cheesy it might seem, love at first sight still existed.

Take the case of our very own Kabir.

He was attracted to Suhani since the very first day when he saw
her from the union room, and over time, 'deliberate' 'coincidental'
morning walks had strengthened their chemistry. Suhani was timid
and was happy to get the care and respect she got from a friend.
Umm, yes – a friend?

She had never got such importance from anyone, not even her
family, forget friends. She was a lovely singer but in most cases, she
was manipulated by her seniors and peers in the music society. She
tried hard to prove herself, but most of the times, she was denied
opportunity. In all likelihood, she was herself underestimating her
talents. Her society members, who were mean and rude, always
demotivated her. The president didn't like her, apparently. DU
has the best resources for all arts, but the fact cannot be ignored
that some societies are dominated by politics and dirty tricks. You
should know how to handle these small nuances if you want to

explore the talent inside you. If you succeed in it, my friend, you have a very long way to go!

It seemed as if Suhani was being hemmed in – by her house, by her passion and by life in general. Then Kabir entered her life, who made sure that every moment that Suhani spent in his vicinity was a happy one. He untangled things for her. Kabir, on the other hand was a figure who was surrounded by groups of friends and acquaintances. Kabir was the centre of attraction and Suhani was his centre of attraction.

He was one of those who didn't fall in love easily, but once love struck, it was the purest and strongest feeling. In the list of his aims, Suhani's happiness had started to become a priority. Yet, they were *just* friends.

Of course stupid, love is not accepted so easily – there should be some drama at least.

The twist in their tale was Suhani's fear, or say peer pressure. She knew Kabir very well; he was a transparent person. He had told her about everything in his life inside out. But Suhani was apprehensive telling him about her background. And well, Kabir never insisted; he was simply elated with the fact that she was with him, for whatever little time it might be.

However, Suhani was aware of the difference and distance between Gurgaon and Kirti Nagar; it wasn't just twenty miles or thirty metro stations apart, but it was culturally and economically distant too. She always kept herself at a safe distance from him. If her heart took her a step ahead, she took two steps back.

Little did she know that Kabir loved her insanely and he would never in his funniest dreams let their friendship be affected because of what people call 'status'. He wasn't a person who would judge her because she belonged to an orthodox family. His love was above all this. All he wanted was that she stays with him – always with her timid hands in his.

Wishes and expectations! Uff!

But, Suhani was apprehensive about sharing her problems. She didn't want sympathy from Kabir. She liked being treated as an equal. She was still thinking about some lost memories and how Kabir had started to bring a change in her life.

Sitting at the base of the black marble pillars at the Yamuna Bank metro station, Suhani wondered about all this. She was constantly distracted. Kabir, who sat next to her, noticed her hesitation and asked, "Suhani, is everything all right?"

When two people are in love, as the world believes, they start understanding even the silence. Kabir too noticed that Suhani was thinking pensively. She answered slowly, keeping her head on his shoulder. She said, "I pray for the day when everything will be fine."

Kabir looked worried. She had never shared anything about her family and the violent household she belonged to. Perhaps it was the first time when Suhani had started a conversation about herself. Kabir, who looked perturbed, for the first time sensed sadness in her voice. He held her palms and she could feel the warmth.

Some moments have the power to let your feelings speak, howsoever hard you try to silence them.

She held those palms tightly as she thought about what had happened in the morning...

7 a.m.
2/7 Kirti Nagar,
West Delhi

Kavya, the eldest daughter of the Shrivastava family had come to visit, and as she always did, was complaining of how she was married off at twenty whereas Suhani was free to attend college. She said, "What kind of life am I living? Nobody cares. And everyone is only worried about Suhani."

As far as I had heard, relations were never measured by money, but when resources were bleak, affection started disappearing. Mr Shrivastava, who was reading the newspaper and sipping his tea, didn't let anything distract him, whereas Suhani, who was putting her books into her bag, pretended that she didn't hear anything. However, what Kavya said had certainly raised the graph of worry for her. Kavya continued, "My brother-in-law is a graduate from Agra University. And my mother-in-law was asking about Suhani…"

As she narrated this to her mother, Suhani got immensely scared. A tear immediately made its way from her eye. She wiped it at one go.

Marriages were supposed to be a synonym to togetherness, but for her, it was a frightening structure which would further rob her of freedom. It signified a burden, it signified lack of a voice – it signified lack of a life for her.

Suhani didn't waste a single minute at home and quickly rushed to wear her sandals. Chintu as always, commented, "Go, Didi. Just a few more days of this college-drama."

Kavya, who was feeding her two-year old toddler, nodded as Suhani ran out of the door. Till the age of nineteen, she hadn't been allowed to take her decisions; she was dependent and she was taught to be dependent. When she asked for help, she was deliberately made to realize how miserably dependent she was. But somewhere she had accepted her family and compromised with the everyday taunts. She had sacrificed everything, but getting married? That was her worst nightmare.

She ran away from her house – an epitome of patriarchal dominance. She rubbed off her sweat with her palm. Her breath was restless, her heart pumped worry.

'What will I do?' she asked herself.

'Why does Kavya hate me so much? Perhaps because she had to marry so early. She is my sister and she should love me like Kabir loves Amaira.

'Chintu is a spoilt brat. But, why does he hate me? Why does everyone hate me?

'I am not a bad singer, but my president hates me too.

'*Whyyyyy?*'

She shouted inside. A tumultuous turmoil took place inside her. She ran until she found an escape in Kabir's company.

The day was tough at college too. The president of the music society had asked everyone to stay back till five for practice. Suhani obviously couldn't, and the president couldn't understand when Suhani tried to explain her strict parents. Suhani, therefore, also suffered the wrath of her co-members. She was a brilliant singer, but unfortunately, nobody heeded her talent at home and in college, she couldn't be present for all the meetings. She was sure she would have to leave the society too. And the terrible moments had made her feel weaker inside. She just felt the need to hold someone; someone she could cling to and forget the rest of the world.

❖

4:30 p.m.
Yamuna Bank, Delhi

"Suhani, you haven't spoken a word in the past half an hour," Kabir said.

He didn't want to know anything; he was there for her even without knowing what was bothering her. She didn't say anything, but tightened her grip on his hands as tears rolled down her eyes. She felt helpless thinking about the marriage proposal. She knew her family could get rid of her by marrying her to Kavya's brother-in-law or anyone existing in this world. She looked miserable.

Kabir wrapped his arms around her and the next moment, she hid herself in him. Kabir was hesitant to make the move, but in this situation, all Suhani needed was a friend to secure her from her insecurities.

Suhani was scared and Kabir could feel the fear. He held her tightly as people who waited for the metro glared at them, but at the moment, all Kabir thought was of the girl who was in his arms. He insisted this time.

"If there is such a big problem, I have to know about it, Suhani. Tell me."

Suhani didn't say anything except, "Just remember this Kabir, nobody loves me. Nobody. Everyone is selfish. A family is supposed to be supportive, but mine would support the vices against me."

Kabir held her face in his hands and said firmly, "One person who loves you madly is in front of you. Then how can you say nobody?"

In the past two months, there hadn't been an official proposal from Kabir and at this point, perhaps it was most needed. Kabir could no longer keep his feelings unsaid.

He had to tell her how much he loved her.

Suhani was miserable and she was clearly insecure. She needed support. She wiped her eyes roughly and said, "Do you even know me well enough to fall in love?"

Kabir replied firmly, "Whatever I know is enough for me to fall in love with you and you know this."

"You don't know anything Kabir and enough is never enough."

Kabir held her by her shoulders and asked looking straight into her eyes, "Only yes or no? Do you love me?"

Suhani turned her face away and replied, "I don't think so."

Kabir looked dejected.

"No problem. Just one last thing before I leave, the world will suppress you till you succumb to it. The moment you take a stand for yourself, everyone else will start respecting you. Be it the metro incidence or anything else, nobody else but you will have to take a stand for yourself. Feminism is just not a theory; practicing it is what makes it work! Remember that. Good bye."

Dejection and the feeling of moving away from someone you have grown so fond of is certainly not something one can accept easily. Kabir had been a winner – he was loved by his colleagues, and his looks and his persona made him one of the most popular faces in college. His sun, however, was Suhani. He really liked her and hearing a 'no' was certainly disturbing. He felt weak as he turned away. Suhani wanted to stop him but she didn't. Economics was playing the game for her. As she got up to leave, Kavya called her up. She said, "Karandeep and my in-laws have come home. Come fast, Suhani."

Kavya had succeeded in getting her in-laws to meet Suhani. Suhani was scared. Kabir's words echoed in her head.

'*...it is only you who can help yourself*'.

She was fretful, but she knew she could face the worse now because the worse had just happened to her. The only person who loved her had gone away.

She was yet again all alone.

However, isolation gave her the power to handle things, once and for all.

Both the souls were dejected. They felt pain. Kabir, had never in his teenage years fallen in love, never had he reciprocated such feelings for someone, but he felt terribly glum when he imagined a life without Suhani. He was close to tears.

That's what's the problem with love. It brings with it some happy and some sad moments too. Offo! Love and its side effects, I tell you! Phew! I think one should just get done with this feeling, at times. But then, beautiful love stories bring me back to writing about it. Ah! It's always complicated!

❖

6 p.m.
2/7 Kirti Nagar,
West Delhi

When Suhani reached home, three aunties dressed in shiny Punjabi salwar kameezes were having tea with her father and mother. Kavya was feeding her toddler and Chintu looked pleased as well. The society which she was a part of was happier when they saw their conventions being followed (nobody cared whether it was right or wrong). The smile that her parents had on their faces was blissful, but the reason behind that smile was that their daughter was succumbing to their patriarchal order. For them, her ability to manage household chores and reproduce children was enough reason to be proud of her. Why did she require to study then, they thought. After all, Mr Shrivastava could save money if she gave up studying, though he wouldn't mind that money being spent on his son's parties. That's the reality of a particular section of our society!

In a corner, near the aunties sat Karandeep. Suhani glanced at them as she took off her sandals.

"There she is! Suhani, come dear," Kavya exclaimed.

Suhani frowned. Mr Shrivastava smiled at her and asked her to sit next to him. She had always done what he asked her, she had always been an obedient (perhaps scared) child. So, like always, she went and sat near him as instructed.

"Beta, Karan has just graduated from Agra. And he wants to take you out for dinner tonight. Go, get ready."

The boy smiled sheepishly and requested, "Please wear blue. I like the colour."

Domination had started even before the relationship was built. The aunties shared some naughty glances. He was a boy, after all. And everything a boy did was justified for them. However, Suhani didn't answer. She asked straight away, "Are you working?"

The aunties looked at her startled.

How dare she ask such a question?

Kavya gestured to Suhani to shut up. Suhani didn't. She asked, "Excuse me, how much do you earn by the way?"

The mother of the boy intervened, "What do you mean? He is still studying in DU."

Suhani gathered some more courage and asked, "Which college, aunty?"

The lady was mum. Of course it was a lie. He was not studying or anything of that sort. Suhani then asked, more confident, "Didi told me you had done your BA in economics, could you tell me a bit about our national income and GDP?"

Everyone looked at her in disbelief.

She had committed a crime by asking the boy some apt questions.

Her mother didn't say anything, but Kavya tried to justify her behaviour.

"Sorry. She is a little tired."

Her mother-in-law retorted, "She is a manner-less girl. We don't want to take her home. Let's go."

'Take her home'. Objectification at its best.

But, Suhani's father stopped everyone and turned to Suhani saying, "What the hell is this? Suhani, touch aunty ji's feet and apologize."

"I won't."

She was no longer a silent object which somebody could 'take' home. She had found her voice.

Soon after, a tight slap landed on her face. She cried in anguish as her petite face stung, but she didn't have anything else to lose. She had already lost Kabir. She said with tears in her eyes, "Hit me again and again, but I will not do anything that I feel is wrong."

The ladies kept murmuring and continued doing so until the drama reached its climax and Suhani's father said, "Either apologize or leave my house. You should know what it is like to be without a shelter. Get out!"

Suhani didn't say anything, but started walking out of the house. She didn't take a single penny along with her. Instead, she took all the money out from her bag and threw it on Chintu's face. She said with fierce anger floating in her eyes, "Now you can shut up every morning. Keep all the money."

And for the first time, without fear in her eyes, she walked out without a single rupee in her hand. She wanted freedom, freedom from everything which bound her – freedom from the misogynistic and patriarchal society. She wanted to be recuperated; she wanted to transgress, *if struggling for one's own identity is termed 'transgressive'.*

The pot of sufferings had reached its brim and Suhani didn't think about anything else but a free life. Anger, frustration, the pain of taking a wrong decision about Kabir, the pain of losing him, the anguish of living a bonded life – all these things had accumulated and forced Suhani to take a stand for herself. Even she knew, if she had not spoken, she would never be able to stand for her identity. Plus, Kabir's words echoed constantly in her mind.

'*...it is only you who can help yourself*'.

However, after walking briskly for an hour, Suhani realized what she had done.

'Where will I go? Where will I stay? What will I eat? The glances of these rowdy men scare me, where will I feel safe?' These were some of the questions which struck her as she sat on the stairs of the Gurudwara. She was scared and she knew just one name which could save her.

She called Kabir, who was watching some comic shows to divert his mind from the sorrow. Suhani said in between sobs, "Can you come and meet me right now?"

Her voice was trembling and she sounded extremely vulnerable. Kabir didn't ask any questions but asked her for the location as he picked up the keys of his car. It was nine at night and the roads were relatively empty. But reaching one end of the city from Gurgaon would take quite a bit of time, yet Kabir drove, not caring for signals, and breaking rules because nothing could stop him from seeing Suhani.

In the meantime, the Shrivastava household seethed with anger. Karandeep, who looked decent but was a misogynist, was offended by the disrespect and decided to teach Suhani a lesson. He left the house and went looking for her.

After half an hour of driving around on his bike, Karandeep found Suhani sitting on the stairs of the Gurudwara. It was a small locality after all. Meanwhile, Kabir had almost reached, but the narrow road inside Kirti Nagar restricted the movement of his SUV. He knew he couldn't take the car any further. He parked it near a shop. It was unusual for him to not care about his SUV – it was his first love, after all. He ran towards the Gurudwara as fast as he could.

Karan came walking towards Suhani, who sat teary-eyed. Suhani saw him and for a moment felt fearful. She didn't react though.

"How much do I earn? What is economics? What is my college? It seems you had decided to insult me. Now I'll tell you Suhani, what being insulted is really like," he snarled.

She was trembling with fear. Strange, no? It seems alien to us, those who live in liberal environment to even imagine this situation, isn't it? But, it does happen. Even today, some people live in the 'society' that they have built, where boys are fit into stereotypical roles of being masculine and strong, but girls are taught to be sensitive and polite. If Suhani was unable to take a stand for herself, it was because fear was imbibed in her since childhood. Why? Why can't we get away with stereotypes?

But, yet again, Kabir's words echoed in her ear.

'*...it is only you who can help yourself*'.

Suhani gathered courage and replied, "You dare touch me. I am telling you... you..."

As she said so, Karandeep came nearer. Every step he took made her pray that Kabir would reach quickly. Kabir, on the other hand, was struggling through the people in the crowded market which smelled of meat and alcohol.

He ran, tracing the Gurudwara on his GPS.

Karan came closer to Suhani and held her by her shoulders, warning her, "You know, I will give you five minutes. Either kneel down and apologize or I'll disrobe you in front of everyone here. You insulted me within four walls. I promise I'll take you back there and what I'll do is something you will repent all your life. Now – at my feet!"

Suhani could smell the alcohol in his breath. She was scared, but kept her courage intact. She jerked her hand from his grip and gave him a tight slap. Kabir by this time could see the Gurudwara.

He saw Suhani slap that man and deep inside his heart he was happy to see her taking a stand for herself. But, the slap certainly didn't go well with the boy. Karandeep held her wrist tightly and said, "Now, you see, you bitc..."

Even before he could complete his sentence, Suhani saw Kabir, who was running towards her. She knew she would be fine.

She bit Karandeep's hand and ran towards Kabir. Karandeep shrieked in pain as he saw Suhani running towards Kabir. Kabir smiled and took her in his arms. She thrust her face on his chest and hid her eyes in him, assuring herself with his heartbeat that everything was fine.

He embraced her as she said, letting her tears flow, "I almost thought you wouldn't reach on time, Kabir."

Kabir smiled, happy at the fact that Suhani was no longer the Suhani he had left behind at Yamuna Bank. He patted her back as the crowd in the marketplace stared. Karandeep walked towards them angrily but Kabir's physique and his angry eyes scared him. He left the place after threatening them. Coward.

The men who self-appoint themselves as superior to women are cowards, after all. If you need her identity to find yours, if you need her body to gratify yours, if you need to snatch her confidence to build yours, my friend, there wouldn't be any identity, but a void that will engulf your life forever. No happiness, but a deep void.

Kabir smiled as he held Suhani by her shoulders and wiped away her tears.

"When you handled the moron so well, how would he dare to touch you?"

Suhani replied, "Y...you saw me..."

"Yes, I did, but I didn't intervene. Somewhere I wanted to see you handle things for yourself at one point of time. I am proud of you. But, how did all this happen?"

Suhani narrated the whole story to Kabir, walking towards the car. Suhani realized how wrong she was when she thought Kabir's love would be affected by her economic status. Kabir, on the other hand, didn't even think a bit about it. For him, she was of utmost importance. Suhani completed her story, "...the point is that I don't even have any shelter. Where am I to go, Kabir?"

I am sure you know where Suhani would go.

Kabir smiled, opening the door of his SUV for her and said, "Come."

He didn't answer any other questions which she threw at him – Where are we going? Where would I stay? etc. Kabir just drove along the comparatively empty highways and roads. As they drove, a serene silence accompanied them. Suhani was tired and put her head back and reclined on the seat.

Suhani sat in the passenger's seat of his SUV, the car he was in love with. He smiled at the fact that she was the first person with whom he was happy to share his car. Otherwise, it was just him and his car – the two madly in love! She stared at the road and said, a little softly, "You are taking me home, right?"

"Absolutely wrong. First we are going for dinner and then home. I am very hungry and I am sure even you must be," he replied.

Kabir was happy to find Suhani identifying herself. He simply smiled angelically.

Suhani replied, "But Kabir, I don't have money. You know this. How can I come with you, plus…"

Kabir interrupted as he drove ahead towards the Ambience Mall. He said, "I owe you many treats. It is one of them. And then, since Amaira left, I have been staying alone and who likes being alone? Don't worry, I'll help you find paid internships. In fact, you could work for our union. So, don't worry, you can pay me back. I would be happy to take the treats back too. Anything that saves me from homemade food is bliss."

Suhani smiled understanding the understanding he had created between them. Kabir said as he parked his car, "Now, if you don't mind, let's rush to the food court before they close?"

Suhani smiled brightly and came along. A little lost, a little happy, a little free, a little caught up, a little in love and with much more respect for the man she was with. They had dinner and drove back to Kabir's house.

He saw the uncomfortable and hesitant reaction on her face as he inserted the keys into the lock of the main door. And as they entered, he clarified, "There's a separate guest room. It's all yours. And I usually am in the drawing room, watching TV. If you need anything, just let me know. Okay?"

Her smile was enough a reaction for Kabir to understand that her doubts were clear. She turned to the guest room but then turned back and stepped towards Kabir. She smiled and gave him a warm hug. As her hands were wrapped around his neck, he could feel the warmth. She felt secure. She whispered with tears in her eyes, "Thank you for everything."

Kabir closed his eyes. He knew it was nothing else but love! He felt her around him. Her hair brushed his face and he could feel the aroma of her perfume. If given a chance, Kabir would freeze the whole world at that very moment, but unfortunately for him, Suhani realized and moved a step back.

Instant attraction is most dangerous.

Awkwardness filled the atmosphere for a moment, but was soon replaced with tranquility. Kabir smiled at her and sat on his bean bag, pretending to watch some news, though all he thought of at that moment was about her – every little moment he spent with her.

Suhani went inside her room and while lying down, even she could think of nothing but him. And the drastic change that happened in her life. Few hours ago, she was scared, fearful and submissive. And now, she wanted to be tameless.

While thinking about Suhani, Kabir felt sad. For once, he tried to think about her life for the past nineteen years. And as he traced her life journey, he thought about the new start she was willing to make.

It would be tough for her, even if she wanted to work. Kabir had assured her that he would help her get internships, but even he knew DU internships didn't pay enough for a person to survive. He was happy to see her free, but her freedom had come at a cost and the journey had just started. 'Would Suhani become independent?' was the question he asked himself while thinking about her. Perhaps yes, perhaps no.

He didn't want to be a protector, he wanted her to be self-dependent. He could easily afford to take care of all her expenses, but he wanted Suhani to find a way to earn and not be financially or emotionally dependent on him. He was fearful it was difficult, but he liked fighting with destiny.

True love doesn't mean being protective, it means letting your love protect themselves.

Ethics of medicine

9 a.m.
12 October 2013
Classroom, SVS, Bhopal

IT IS SAID, TRANSITIONS ARE DIFFICULT. BUT, SOMETIMES IF one stays strong for a little while, the journey can be fruitful. This realization came to me just a day ago. I was travelling on a flight from Delhi to Indore and minutes before the aircraft was about to take off, the plane started to take the run up at a very high speed. I sat with my eyes closed as I felt uncomfortable. My stomach wasn't reacting very positively to the increasing speed of the aircraft and the cooling inside the craft wasn't sufficient in the 49 degree heat of Delhi. I kept my eyelids closed as the aircraft took the transition from the ground to the sky and within five minutes from the takeoff, I started feeling better. In no time I was enjoying my flight between the clouds with some coke and nachos!

You know what? Every transition shall pass and slowly settle, just keep yourself intact.

Life works similarly. Look at our very own Amaira. She didn't have the best of starts, but was happy in the world she was in now. In fact, Amaira had started to gain the traits of a nerd.

Dr Raghuvanshi, her favourite teacher, who had staunchly hated her in the beginning, had started to trust her with responsibilities now. Although he always scolded her for wearing short dresses in college, the stubborn streak in Amaira didn't let her change even a bit. Slowly, Amaira became habitual of the harsh words in class. She had slowly started to adapt to the adverse conditions.

And for Mr Raghuvanshi, he saw a spark in Amaira's skills and for the first time, *his conventional thinking was overridden by talent*. So basically, some changes were welcoming.

That day, Dr Raghuvanshi was taking a lecture on the ethics of medical sciences. He was talking about the various responsibilities a doctor holds while he is inside an operation theatre.

"So, the first ethic is to let the patient know everything. Keep the words simple, but make sure you mention all the facts when you talk to your patient…"

Amidst his lecture, he always added some personal experiences which made the concepts more realistic. No wonder he was so well admired among his students. As he taught, Amaira heard each and every word of his with dedication and kept jotting down notes. Precisely that dedication had melted Raghuvanshi sir's conventional thoughts, or at least had started to. Just when he was wrapping up the lecture and taking the roll call, he said concluding his lecture, "And well, these were the ethics of medicine. However, little do some students know about discipline. They wish to treat patients in miniskirts. Anyway, that's how the generation today is…"

As he spoke, Amaira smirked and said to herself, 'and he starts again'!

She was aware that there was a taunt in store for her. In fact, she appreciated Raghuvanshi sir's wit because he brought unique ideas to target her every day. The class too, enjoyed those comments and jokes in light humour. However, Arjun never appreciated the jokes at Amaira's expense. And Amaira didn't care. Trust, it is said, once lost is lost like a ring in sand dunes. Rajbir, who sat on the adjacent table whispered to Amaira, "Pulse is round the corner. Trish and I have registered for you as well."

Alright! So, Pulse was something every medical student was aware of.

The annual fest of AIIMS, Delhi. The perfect combination of glamour, glitter and exposure, Pulse was a nine-day festival. And even far off medical colleges prepared a lot for giving performances. SVS was certainly one of those.

Amaira winked and said, "It'd be fun to go back home."

However, Rajbir burst her bubble of staying at her luxurious house in Gurgaon.

"Home? But we'll be staying in AIIMS."

"Definitely not. I will stay with my brother. I am done with this hostel life," she retorted.

"No. You will miss so much fun. We all are planning a *Dilli darshan* too – will visit all the monuments and markets. Most of our friends haven't ever been to Delhi before," he explained.

"Rajbir, stop pretending as if you haven't ever visited any monument or market in Delhi. The simpler thing is that you want to spend some cozy time with your girlfriend. So, have fun. I'll stay at home."

Amaira was hard to convince, but Rajbir tried and tried until he succeeded. Amaira agreed to stay with her friends in the hostels, sacrificing the luxuries of her five star house.

Amaira got up to leave, but turned around and asked, "When are we leaving for Delhi?"

"The sooner the better. In ten days."

Amaira nodded as she walked outside the classroom, thinking about her tickets and accommodation in AIIMS. Just then, she saw Kushank – her (*I think*) friend. He was talking over phone, but seeing her, his heart skipped a few beats. She looked cheerfully beautiful.

Being herself, she waved at him enthusiastically and smiled broadly. She thought of him as a friend after all. But Kush took a step back and moved in the opposite direction. The mere thought of being friendly with a student in college was so stereotypical and typical. The gaze of the others stopped him from meeting her. He knew it wouldn't go well with everyone. He just walked away and went inside his cocoon.

After the Council inspections, Kushank was a happier person. Accomplishment, it is said, brings with it confidence and strength. Amaira had left a noticeable impact on him. He was confident of managing his business along with the hospital. Amaira was a confidence booster, not only for him, but for most of her friends. But did Kushank acknowledge the fact?

Could a person who never acknowledged himself acknowledge someone else?

Wasn't he being mean by ignoring her in front of everyone? What is friendship if one is hesitant to acknowledge being friends?

Can friendship be friendship if it was embarrassing for any one of them?

Certainly, Amaira noticed the change in Kushank. He was playing a dual game with her – at one level he was friendly and close to her, and at another he completely ignored her. Amaira didn't bother, but didn't fail to notice his reaction. He on the other hand was living quadruple personalities: he loved her but he was too messed up to confess, he was scared. He wanted to be with her, but what others would say mattered more than his happiness to him. He was just confused, *as always*.

He was, in fact, leaving Bhopal for fifteen days as he had some urgent work in Delhi. As Amaira had filled him with confidence, he started to believe in himself and challenge limitations.

I wonder though, how long would he try? Or manage?

In the fifteen days he was away, neither he nor Amaira sent text messages like they used to. Amaira almost forgot about what had happened; she was instead dating her books. Meanwhile, Kushank and Vishesh launched a new game, whose marketing Kush was handling brilliantly. He belonged to that world. And he started to feel satisfied.

It's true, when one does what they really want, the day ends with an unparalleled satisfaction. And trust me, no project target or financial target could match that!

❖

6 a.m.
27 October 2013
SVS gym, Bhopal

Without being forgetful, I am sure I did mention in bold words that Amaira was a foodie. The girl grabbed everything that was considered junk. And, she loved sweets. And with such an appetite for food, apart from her genes, the other thing which kept her slim and fit was her workout. Initially, she was too tired with the hectic classes, but gradually she started working out daily. SVS had a gym which wasn't as luxurious as her gym back home, but it worked well for the hostelers. Stay in a hostel and you'll learn all the survival strategies. Though it bonds you with a few friends for lifetime, it is exhausting.

Every morning, Amaira would be the first one to enter the gym. It was in her peculiar traits to be stubborn. *She didn't even leave the poor fats alone.* It was just another day for Amaira when she was running on the treadmill. Dressed in a sports tank top and a skin fit lower, she tied her hair in a high bun and was running at a speed of eight kilometres per hour. She slowly increased her speed and continued to run faster. She had burnt 1350 calories and her pulse was 110 according to the screen on the treadmill.

She had already completed six kilometres, but she liked crossing her boundaries.

She always wanted more.

On the other hand, the trustee was back in the campus. Kush had returned by a night flight from Delhi and was all set to come back and take the entire workload on his tiresome back. He entered the gates of SVS, driving swiftly. Parking the car in its usual place, Kushank made his way to his cabin.

He had been awake all night, working on the details of a controversial case in the hospital. He had been issued a notice by the medical authorities and he had to sort the case as soon as possible. Kushank had learnt one thing – running a hospital brought its own share of controversies for free!

And slowly, he was learning to handle them.

Or maybe, he thought he was handling everything right!

But, as he walked the empty corridors, he felt serenity around him. He could feel the rays of the sun which peeped in through the arched corridors, and he could feel the air flowing freely through the windows in the corridors. For the first time, he found tranquility in college and in his life. Kushank, for once, forgot about the notice, the cases, the audit – everything.

He closed his eyes and felt the breeze on his face. A thought passed his mind; he wanted to thank Amaira. He wanted to thank the reason because of whom he was able to manage both his dream as well as his responsibilities. He blamed the atmosphere for reminding him about her. In Delhi, she would just be a thought, but here, when she was around, she became a distraction. Well, a positive distraction to be precise. And just when Kushank was breathing in the tranquil atmosphere…

"Aaaargh!"

The sound of someone yelling in pain suddenly startled him. The bubble of peace around him burst immediately. Startled and worried, Kushank followed the voice.

It had come from the gym.

While working out, Amaira had ambitiously increased the speed of the treadmill when her shoe lace got entangled in the belt of the running machine. Amaira was thrown off the machine.

Kushank entered the gym and saw her on the floor. He ran towards her.

Amaira was synonymous with problems, he thought. He didn't wait for a second and switched off the main switch and then helped Amaira get up. She was injured. Her left shoe lace was entangled in the rubber belt and her right knee was bleeding profusely because of its friction with the fast moving belt.

Everything Amaira did had a tadka of the dramatic. She perhaps didn't take anything 'normally' – not even a little scratch. Then, this was something magnificently worrying. She cried in pain. Kushank, who stood baffled, was still trying to figure out how the peace had been transgressed into chaos around him.

He loved her and books have said tons about how a person in love cannot see his love in pain, blah blah! Well, similar was the feeling Kushank was going through. He couldn't bear to see her in pain. Kushank immediately searched for a first aid box in the cupboards of the gym and then, applied some antiseptic to her wounds. Amaira shrieked in pain, "Have you lost it? It's paining a lot!"

Amaira couldn't or didn't want to tolerate pain. Kushank meekly replied, "I have applied some ointment, Amaira."

While he helped her, he also took a look around, ensuring that no one saw them.

He was hell concerned about 'others'. At times, I just lose my head over this fellow! Ah, moving on...

Amaira screamed, "I am talking about my left ankle. It's paining a lot."

Kushank quickly removed her shoes and pressed her ankle. Amaira shouted. Kushank grasped from the pain that it was a serious sprain or dislocation. He quickly applied a pain relieving spray to her ankle, after which he helped her to stand. Unfortunately, all his efforts were in vain. Amaira was going through intense pain and she was unable to stand because of the excruciating pain.

She kept sitting there on the floor. Just like a two-year-old, she looked at him with a puppy face. Kushank could feel her pain looking at her big drops of tears. He had an urge to forget everything and give her a tight hug, but he restrained himself, *as always*. He cupped her face in his palms and wiped away the tears, explaining, "Look at me. You are fine. Just relax."

His calmness was all washed away at once when Amaira began to scream, "What the hell? It's paining. Don't you understand? Stop giving me a motivational speech."

Kushank knew Amaira was impulsive. She wouldn't think before she reacted, and right now, her ankle wouldn't even let her think. Kushank searched for a pain killer in the first aid box and checked the expiry date. He brought water and helped Amaira take the medicine. She protested as Kushank carefully held the tablet, "I want a syrup."

"What?"

"I want a syrup."

"Come again?" he asked, amused.

"Sir, I said I don't like tablets. Get me some syrup. *Go!*"

"Shut up Amaira. I think the pain has separated your brain from your head. You are not a little child. Come on, have this now."

Amaira resisted. Kushank softened and said, "Okay, listen. You are afraid of tablets, right?"

"No," she disagreed. He held her pointing hand and continued, "Okay, you are not. Then, statue!"

He smartly took the glass and the tablet and served the girl with his hands. Kushank, however, went a step ahead in being dramatic. After giving her the medicine, he asked her to lie down and he, being the only one around at such an early hour, helped her exercise her ankle slowly. Even he didn't know why he was so caring towards her. Or perhaps he knew, but was trying not to accept it.

We know it though!

Amaira asked, "What were you doing here?"

Surely, Amaira had started feeling better as she forgot about her pain for the moment.

I was thinking about you, Kushank wanted to reply, but as always, he hid his true feelings and said, "I had just returned from Delhi and a few cases needed my attention urgently."

Amaira smiled for the first time after the dramatic fall. She then said, quite unlike of Amaira, "Sir, thank you."

'Thank you?' Kushank wondered.

For the very first time, he felt a bond blossoming between them. Amaira too was thankful to him for being by her side. Kushank smiled back and asked her, shyly eyeing her, "How is the pain? If you can walk a bit now, let's go and get it checked in the dispensary."

"No, I'll be fine."

'Don't call me sir, Kush sounds better,' he thought looking at her fine features.

Strangely, it was always after overreacting that Amaira realized that she was fine.

Kushank helped her get up and walk to the corner, after which he walked towards his cabin. He checked with his office staff about the reports.

It took some time for him to concentrate on his work after spending so many moments with the biggest distraction of his life. Amaira on the other hand struggled to walk to her room and lay down. Roop helped her by bringing breakfast inside the room and by helping Amaira with medicines. Yet, what rest could do for her, nothing else could. Amaira missed the day's classes and relaxed, playing some of her favourite movies on her laptop.

Amaira was watching some boring series on her laptop, when her phone buzzed.

'I hope you are better.'

The message was from Kushank.

Amaira replied formally, 'Of course, I am good. Thank you.'

The receiver perhaps didn't check the Messenger and therefore, the reply came by mid-afternoon.

'Tablets aren't that bad Amaira.'

Amaira checked and thought of a witty reply. She typed, then erased, then typed again.

'Might be, but only in good company.'

It wasn't the first time she was texting, but it was certainly the first time when she thought before touching the send button. Anyhow, the day ended with an injured Amaira, who had missed Raghuvanshi sir's class too because she was hardly able to move.

His taunts must have gone wasted for the day, eh?

Later, she took all the notes from Roop and heard about the day at college. Roop mentioned, "Amu, you know about that couple's list?"

Amaira remembered Rini's friend mentioning about it.

"Yeah! These kids haven't grown up yet."

"Exactly, and you know, they are planning to put up the list by tomorrow midnight. It's shocking how almost everyone in college is talking about it. I just feel weird."

"Let it be. Neither of us is going to be affected by the list. So, for me, what's more important is whether your mum sent those *pinnis*?" Amaira asked.

Pinni is a delicious Punjabi sweet and Roop's mother was a master chef. Amaira being Amaira had a very good connection with Roop's mother and she had rightfully demanded her favourite sweet. Amaira savoured them, and while eating, they talked about Pulse, and the trip.

With some thoughts buzzing around her like they always did, Amaira tried to sleep.

Kushank was sleep deprived, though. He drove back close to midnight and went to bed without eating anything. Mrs Khanna was happy to see Kush, her young son being responsible and strong. She could see he was as confident as her now.

I wish she was right.

He got into bed and just before he dozed off to sleep, a frame was immediately formed in his mind and he saw the moment at the gym. But, he immediately shooed the thoughts away. She was *just* a student and he was the owner of the college where she studied. He was eight years elder to her and...

...ignoring the thoughts was much easier than to face the harsh truth of reality!

There's a feeling in the air –
and it's called love

4:25 p.m.
5 November 2013
North Campus, Delhi University

THE HEAT IN THE ATMOSPHERE HAD LESSENED, THE HUMIDITY
had started to bid adieu to the city and a calm breeze had replaced
the hot summer wind. The sun was warm but the breeze kept it
cool. The city was looking beautiful as autumn descended. The
students of DU were ready to sit for another semester examination
in December. Third year had in fact been adventurous for Kabir.

Politics, academics and his ambitions – there was a sense
to achieve everything at one go. Third year does that to you
deliberately – you feel the world's coming to an end after a few
months run for entrances, placements and enter the complexities of
the world! Competition is one word I am sure you think of again
and again then.

The last year in college brings a sense of responsibility and with
his political ambitions standing high, Kabir wanted to stay on in
DU. His sole purpose was to make a prominent place for himself in

137

one of the leading parties. However, Suhani's entry was a pleasant surprise! And the past one month had simply been like a fairy tale for him. He and Suhani would come to college together, go back together and at home, he would be glad to be in the company of the girl he loved. Suhani, who had started working for two internships, was happy to be in a space where she felt important.

Fairy tales are beautiful, and we love them, don't we?

Yes, staying in such luxury wasn't something which she had experienced before. She did take time adjusting to the way in which Kabir lived – everything was a call away.

However, no two people are similar. Quarrels, arguments and fights are inevitable. At times, Kabir would just get irritated at how dependent Suhani was. He had always seen independent women in his mother and Amaira, but Suhani was miserably dependent expecting him to be with her, if possible every minute of her life.

She had to be independent. If she hadn't learnt, she would have to learn and that was the key to their conflict.

This morning too, a similar disagreement took place and the two went their own ways. Kabir went to the union room and sat with a terrible temper whereas Suhani looked upset. Even while rehearsing for the upcoming fests with her society, she could not focus.

Transgressing from the patriarchal beliefs and the rules of the Shrivastava household had proved beneficial for her. She was free to rehearse, take part in as many events as she could and practice till late hours. Kabir would always wait for her. And her position in her college's music society strengthened. The not-so-wonderful society members all of a sudden started respecting Suhani. In fact, she was representing her college in one of the solo singing events as well. But it required her to practice day and night. Even that day, after a few rehearsals, Suhani forgot about the little argument she had had with Kabir.

On the other hand, Kabir realized his fault. He was being too harsh on the timid person he loved. He called Suhani n number of times but because her phone was kept away from her while rehearsing, she didn't hear it. The lack of communication between them made Kabir apprehensive. He thought that it was anger which prevented her from picking up the call. And to make up for the loss, he walked to her college and entered slyly through the back gate.

This wasn't him generally, but Bollywood tells us love is magical, it can transform anyone! (Spare me for the clichéd stuff, though.)

In between this, Amaira called and for the first time, Kabir's priority was Suhani. He didn't pick up the phone and entered the college premises to look for Suhani. He knew Suhani would be around the auditorium or the back lawns.

Absolutely correct! She was there in the dimly-lit auditorium.

Kabir walked hastily to the door but when he saw her sing, he stopped. Looking at her and hearing her beautiful voice echoing in the empty auditorium, Kabir forgot the world he lived in. He was mesmerized.

He stood still, without even letting a heartbeat thud. It seemed to him that the world paused for a minute. Her simplicity, her eyes, her voice – he wanted to tell her how much he loved her. He just couldn't stop himself.

'Why don't I tell her?' he questioned himself.

'What if she leaves the house if she doesn't feel the same?' his counter self retorted.

'No but, I love her. I should tell her,' he repeated.

'As you wish then. Don't crib when she leaves,' the counter-Kabir argued.

Kabir stood there and shooed away the thoughts.

He was well enough in love to be confused. *However, emotions are always a maze to get lost in.* He just looked at her until his steps started moving in her direction. He wanted to stop but his heart couldn't.

He just walked up to her and in the dim golden light of the empty auditorium, gave her a tight hug.

Feelings are very stubborn, at times you just can't control yourself!

Suhani was taken aback. What had happened to him all of a sudden, she wondered.

She stood there, instructing her heart to be distant from the feeling she was nervous of. Kabir didn't say anything, nor did Suhani. Perhaps heartbeats were enough for them. Kabir forgot everything for a moment, and when he opened his eyes, he immediately loosened his grip on Suhani.

Suhani smiled bleakly, controlling the hundred butterflies inside her stomach. Suhani had lived so many emotions in that touch. She felt Kabir's care, his affection, his admiration...and his love.

She felt secure in those arms, but perhaps she was a bit apprehensive of her feelings.

No words came between them that day.

She smiled as they walked towards the metro station on the empty roads of North Campus. They had walked the road many times, but it wasn't ever as beautiful as it was that day. Kabir had lived in the campus for three years and yet, for the first time, the campus looked mesmerizing!

Suhani too, had never felt what she was feeling.

There was a difference in the oxygen they breathed in. As they walked, the laws of attraction were playing a very crucial role. As their steps moved ahead, their palms brushed against one another. It sent a tickling sensation down their spines; Suhani hid a blush immediately.

Kabir, tired of fighting with his emotions, didn't try to hide them. He smiled and looked at her. She turned away her gaze deliberately.

Her heart skipped a beat when her palms brushed against his. And while taking a step ahead, Kabir's palms touched hers again and this time, without missing a moment, he held her hand. *Till when can you fight with feelings? For once, they'll win.*

World's red color had all of a sudden started to vanish because all of it was collected on her cheeks. She felt so many feelings at one go and trying very hard to defend all these emotions, she still hid her feelings.

And in between the comparatively empty roads, the calm breeze, and overall blissful atmosphere, their fingers had entwined silently, promising to stay in each other's company. As they walked ahead, Suhani slyly slid her hands away when she saw the metro queue. Kabir smiled as he moved ahead. For him, it was everything he had thought about, imagined about.

Every night before he slept, he saw her glittering eyes and had always imagined so many moments with her – holding her hand, being with her and what not. *Imaginations, ah!* He was certainly in a different space. Suhani, who walked to the women's line, went through many emotions deep in her heart. While the female guard was frisking her, she was blushing profusely. She walked ahead and picked up her bag from the scanning machine and then, looking down, she walked beside Kabir. The spark, as I said, had been lit and the two were very much in the feeling which we commonly call *love*.

Words were absent, yet so many meanings flowed around!

❖

Soon they were in the train. Holding the side steel rod for support, Suhani stood amidst crowded passengers and Kabir stood inches away from her. In between the journey, the jerks would bring them closer. Suhani would say nothing, but blush a deep red. Her smile blossomed unconditionally.

As the metro voyaged forward from Central Secretariat to Udyod Bhavan, the lights dimmed a bit as they always did, but that day, Kabir's heart instructed his actions. His hands slowly slid down the steel rod which was held by Suhani and he kept his palm over hers. Every feeling was new, every expression novel.

The feelings were simple, yet immensely complicated. In a second, they felt a mélange of emotions. In the messaging language, it would have been difficult using a single emoji for the expressions they were feeling at the moment. Together, in one go, they felt everything. Precisely the passion, the care, the love, the tenderness, the admiration, the craving for love, the happiness, the confusion, the spark, the touch, and above everything, the togetherness. Kabir looked at her fondly which she reciprocated for the first time.

The day had all of a sudden taken a U turn. Both of them had been in each other's company but had not felt the way they felt for each other that day. As they walked back home, there were so many unsaid feelings which they went through while taking each step towards their nest. Suhani smiled and as they entered the lift, for the first time, gathering courage and listening to what her heart said, she timidly put forward her hand and held his.

No words, yet.

Kabir was more than elated. For the first time, he knew her answer.

And strangely, without uttering a single word, the feelings had played the game for them. Kabir and Suhani entered home and just when they were entering the house, Kabir checked the letter box. There was one. It was for Suhani.

"Did you apply for an internship, Suhani?"

When he was talking about work, Kabir would forget about everything else. Akaash and Preeti had always taught their kids to keep work above everything in life. Kabir's voice was serene yet serious as he handed the letter to Suhani. Suhani opened it ecstatically and jumped after reading it, "Oh my god! This is such good news!"

Kabir didn't know anything about it. He was just happy to see her happy. She exclaimed with joy, giving him a tight hug.

"There is a workshop for vocal training by Bollywood's well-known music directors. I had filled the online application trying my luck. I had sent an audio CD of my voice. Just imagine, they replied and I am among the top fifty applicants to be selected for the workshop."

Kabir was overwhelmed. He genuinely wanted the best for Suhani, but he never knew of all her achievements in her field. Until that day, he hadn't even know about her beautiful voice. She, perhaps, underestimated her achievement or perhaps she was never motivated about her singing.

"Whoa! That is big! Congratulations. You are so talented."

"No, no!" Suhani struggled.

Kabir said, holding her shoulders, "Suhani, trust me, you will be one of the best singers in the country."

She wished she was as confident about herself as Kabir was. She read the letter once again, and then Suhani said, worried, "This workshop is in Mumbai. How am I gonna go there alone?"

Kabir, who was busy calling Anuriti and Raghav to invite them for a quick dinner to celebrate Suhani's success, looked up at her. He immediately left his phone as he walked towards her. He sat beside her and said, keeping his palm over hers, "Suhani, everybody has to find their way alone. They will arrange for your stay there. You don't need to worry."

He winked.

Suhani sighed. She had never stepped out of her boundaries. Blame her upbringing or her personality, she had never even tried to challenge her own limitations. She was afraid of moving out. She was apprehensive and looking at her nervousness, Kabir said, "Why do you always under-estimate yourself? Learn to trust yourself. You are much much more talented than you think you are."

Suhani obviously wasn't convinced, but looking at Kabir's happiness, she didn't argue. After all, it wasn't about him or anybody else; she knew it was her personality and only she could win over it. She smiled and went inside to get ready. As she moved towards the guest room, she asked with a smirk, "Are we going on a date?"

Kabir smiled and replied with a grin, "Sure, with Raghav and Anuriti."

Suhani smiled and went inside. It was so unlike her to ask a question like that, Kabir thought. He went inside as well to get ready.

Kabir had always seen Suhani in simple suits. She never left her hair open, she never applied any artifice and was always simple. Beautifully simple. But, as I said, the day was special. Celebrations had to be different.

Suhani, after taking half an hour to get ready, hadn't come out yet. Kabir had already knocked thrice. He stood outside the guest room, waiting for his 'date' and knocked for the fourth time, almost sounding impatient, "Suhani, Raghav and Anuriti would kill me for keeping them waiting together. You know that they are not on talking terms. Just imagine! Poor hotel people, I am already feeling sorry for them."

Suhani, who was applying the last brush of her eye liner, smiled at herself in the mirror. It seemed as if she was meeting her new self. She smiled and got up to unlock the door. Kabir, who was waiting restlessly for Suhani for once couldn't believe his eyes.

Suhani was dressed in a red knee-length dress. Her hair was curly and for the first time, she had left her shoulder-length hair open. They looked pretty with some pins tying them perfectly. Her eyes, the most honest part of her face was lined with kohl and her lips were brushed with a shiny gloss. For the first time perhaps, Suhani met this side of hers. She was always fond of getting dressed, but at home applying just some kohl became a matter of great concern. She never thought of being beautiful. But she was and Kabir couldn't help but simply stare at her continuously. Suhani, who looked graceful, said, looking at the handsome hunk standing in front of her, "Let's leave. Even you look nice."

Kabir was startled by her voice as he came out of his thoughts. He then, tried to recall what he wore. It was a formal blue shirt with black chinos. His ruffled hair was the most attractive part of his face. Suhani brushed her fingers through them. And every moment that she came closer to him was golden.

"You look gorgeous," he said, looking at her with dreamy eyes.

She smiled. A blush was supposed to accompany it. It certainly did. She replied with a smile, "Aren't we getting late now?"

Kabir thought for a while, 'I wish I had not called Raghav and Anu! It would have been a perfect date!'

They both came down to the car and got seated. Just as Kabir revved up the car, his phone buzzed. He was sure Anuriti would kill him for being so late. Anuriti and Raghav, were still not on talking terms and leaving two horrible creatures together wasn't a very safe idea. Kabir asked Suhani to pick the phone and keep it on loud speaker as he drove. As expected, Anuriti shouted over the phone, "Kabir! I am going back. What the hell is this? I have been waiting here with this person. It's difficult."

You remember their equation, don't you?

Suhani looked at Kabir and gave the 'as-expected' smile.

"Anu, it's me. Suhani. Actually, it wasn't his fault. I got late. We'll be there in ten minutes."

What could one say when Suhani spoke in a melodiously sweet voice. Kabir smirked knowing Anuriti well. She wouldn't argue now.

"I am waiting on the table that Kabir booked, with this stranger. Come fast!"

Raghav was being addressed as the stranger. Raghav called Kabir a few minutes later.

"What dude? I have to wait with this girl. I am tired of..."

Anuriti shouted, "How dare you? Egoistic dumbhead."

"EGO?" Raghav said, shocked. Anuriti retorted, "Yes, two months and you didn't find a way to talk to me?"

"Yes, sure Anu. I called you, texted you and even came home, but when all I get is a locked door on my face, how am I supposed to handle things?"

Kabir and Suhani were the mute audience in this conversation. Suhani looked at Kabir and said, "Here they go. I am sure they'll break a glass or two."

"Let them. I have a feeling that this confrontation would make things better for them. They needed this fight, to be frank. Let them fight their hearts out. At least they'll accept what destiny has in store for them."

As they drove, Raghav and Anuriti had a fun time, fighting like kids studying in class three. Somewhere, they were best friends and were only best friends. Feelings and emotions didn't go very well with them.

Some relations, therefore are meant to be as they are created. While some achieve a newer pedestal, some are created to be carried as they are. Anuriti and Raghav were infatuated with each other and they thought it was friendly love (of course, the teasing added to their misconception), they went through a misunderstanding phase and didn't speak for two months, but in their hearts they missed a best friend. And perhaps, Suhani's make-up had helped them get together.

Many times, we don't know when it's love, or when it isn't. Some relations can click in a second and some can go on for ages but still lack love. Love, ah the complicated kid of the class.

Both of them accepted the fact that they were best suited as best friends.

When Kabir and Suhani entered the restaurant, they saw Anuriti and Raghav sitting with sheepish smiles. Thank god!

Kabir expected the two to be fighting with barbeque rods; instead, they were sipping from their soups. Kabir was happy seeing the two together after a very long time. He smiled as he walked with Suhani, saying, "You are lucky. The day has been so lucky for us."

Suhani, who walked with her hand in Kabir's, smiled and said, "We are lucky."

Aha! The Us and We conversations had started. Interesting!

And just as they walked to the table, both Raghav and Anuriti looked at Suhani with their mouths open.

"Man! Suhani, I never knew you could look so hot!"

Raghav added, "Exactly. A completely new avatar."

Kabir smiled at them, so did Suhani.

"Alright. You guys tell us what's up with you two?" asked Kabir.

Grinning, they narrated their story while sampling the best barbeque snacks.

Personally, even I love grilled veggies! My mouth just started watering. Food I tell you! How can one be from Indore and not be a foodie? That's supposed to be impossible, right?

It was a day to be celebrated. Love had penetrated into their lives, making it a better – perhaps a much better place to be in! Friends were back to being friends, keeping love aside for a while and new opportunities stood knocking on the door for Suhani. The dinner marked the reiteration of friendship and a new journey of love for them! Happiness was healing all the open wounds.

Everything seemed perfect and in place. But, was it truly that blissful for Suhani?

❖

It was eleven when the friends wrapped up their treat and Kabir drove home. Suhani, sitting right next to him, looked outside. There had been a drizzle in Gurgaon and the city looked calmer, more peaceful than it was. In fact, it's a personal observation that Gurgaon is a city which glows at night. And while driving back home, the city presents to you the most tranquil *you*. Suhani sat back, relaxed and looked peacefully at the water droplets on the roads. She kept observing how every drop was been driven upon, how freedom comes at a cost.

"How about some tea?" Kabir asked.

Suhani looked around. There wasn't a café for tea or coffee, there wasn't a restaurant either. She replied, "Where?"

Kabir smiled and pointed at a tea vendor. Suhani smiled. By now Kabir had realized that Suhani liked tea, not coffee, which was his favourite. She never said anything when they went for coffees. It was always him who had to decipher the secrets of her choices.

Kabir got down and got two cups of hot tea. When Suhani took the cup from him, her palms were secured by his. Suhani blushed. The day had been kind to her. Kabir and Suhani, while sipping from their tea, looked happy. Kabir asked, "When do you have to leave?"

He had unknowingly brought her back to the topic from which she was running away. She had apprehensions and insecurities, and was nervous deep inside, but managed to reply. And just when Kabir was stepping out of the car to return the cups, Suhani held his wrist and instantly gave him a tight hug.

The nervousness was speaking and Suhani was drenched in fear. Her hands simply didn't want to open the lock of arms which she had built around Kabir; she didn't want to look up, and she just didn't want to leave him. He was her torch in the dark and walking without light was impossible for her, or so she thought.

Kabir smiled in a playful manner and said, "Suhani, people are watching us. Leave me."

People, eh?

Suhani left him immediately and looked embarrassed. She simply looked away and entered the house of her thoughts. It wasn't easy for her to walk into a new space, that too alone. The workshop was a once in a lifetime opportunity but Suhani was more nervous than excited. After reaching home, lying in bed and staring at the white ceiling, she thought about her journey. She had never stepped out and knew she wasn't that strong to handle any kind of pressure alone. In fact, even the decision to walk out of her house was not solely hers. Had Kabir not been there, Suhani would have fallen, she thought. She wanted to, but wasn't able to trust herself.

Why, I wonder at times, do we resist to trust ourselves – aise ho gaya toh? Waise ho gaya toh? *What if? What if not? We are capable of much more than we really think we are. The key is just to let yourself free and find your true capabilities!*

She wanted to, but wasn't able to walk out of the boundaries which life had created around her. She tried to be strong, but something stopped her. Perhaps, nothing else but herself stopped her from being what she could be. Many times, it's nothing but the small fear inside us.

She wasn't able to sleep and Kabir saw it from the door. He saw her uncomfortable and restless, but he didn't enter her space. He wanted her to figure some things about herself, all by herself. He did not try and influence her decision, but left it to her. The workshop was a symbol of strength, confidence and zeal for Suhani. If she wanted to chase her dream, she had to step out of the boundaries she had created for herself. *Once in life, we all have to step out of our comfort zones.*

She thought about it all night long. She confronted her fear; she thought to herself that if it was about taking a chance, why not? Suhani, for once, didn't think about Kabir, her love for him, his care and protection towards her; she thought about herself.

And at times, being a little selfish is not that bad. (Wink!)

After a continuous courtroom hearing in her mind, the defense lawyer won. *She won.*

As the first ray of sunlight entered through the window, she walked out of her room and saw the letter again. She took Kabir's laptop and submitted her confirmation. And in seconds, she received further details from the institute. She smiled at herself and looked at the new, stronger person in her. When Kabir came out of his room, that he saw Suhani fiddling with his laptop and surfing the website for more details. She looked excited. And that was the moment when he had won too. He saw the zeal in her eyes for the first time. Kabir smiled and went inside, letting Suhani be. The roads had cleared themselves of the debris of burden, the stones of under-confidence and the hurdles of self-doubt. Suhani believed in herself now. Confidence had hugged her with warm and open arms.

One moment of self-confrontation can change the way we look at life – or perhaps how life looks at us!

Hospital Diaries

BACK IN BHOPAL, LET'S START FROM WHERE WE HAD STOPPED. Life had taken a dramatic turn for Amaira, as always, and she was ready to face them with the same strength. It strikes me that her life brought happiness, but never satisfaction. It always brought hurdles her way to jump over. She would have an adventurous as well as a struggling life, I feel. Her journeys had more thorns, but the happy part was that Amaira still moved ahead, with some bruises perhaps, but the journey never ended for her! But, do you know the best part about her? She refused to stop. That made her who she was, after all.

7 a.m.
28 October 2013
Kushank's Cabin, SVS, Bhopal

Mornings are supposedly the most delicious starters to the main course of the day. With the perfect amount of hardworking salt, positive pepper and zealous spices, this start works wonders. It was just the same for Kushank. He had lost out on quite a bit about the hospital affairs when he had gone to Delhi.

He sat with Mr Kumar and asked him to brief him about the hospital's progress. As I mentioned before, SVS was a place of changing scenarios. Things, people, situations and luck changed in the blink of an eye.

Mr Kumar looked into a few files and showing the details to Kushank, said, "Sir, the policy which you proposed, that of a loan, is working. The patients are satisfied and we have seen an increase in the patients from lower backgrounds. And the loans are regular."

This was exactly the point of conflict in the hospital when Kushank had suggested the change. He had proposed that those patients who could not afford to pay the bill at one go, should be given a chance to pay in installments and the bill could be deducted from their bank accounts every month. The hospital would not go into any losses, but they would win over the trust of many patients. This way, not only the patients would be comfortable, but they would be loyal to the hospital as well. Initially what seemed as an emotional, immature and sensitive step, now seemed feasible. *Kushank smelled business in everything. For that matter, he was a perfect businessman.*

Kushank replied with a smile, "It should be working, sir. What about the audit of the equipments? Have we got it done?"

"Almost. In fact, everything is on track, except a few cases. There were minor tiffs between the office staff and Dr Kashish day before yesterday. I was thinking of issuing a notice to Dr Kashish for the indiscipline towards hospital rules."

Kushank heard Mr Kumar thoughtfully, after which he said, "No, there's no need. I'll speak to Kashish."

Mr Kumar looked at Kushank with surprise. He had wanted to question him, but he knew Kushank wouldn't answer, so he left. Kushank, on the other hand, trusted Dr Kashish. He knew she was a qualified as well as a responsible doctor. In fact, she had stood by him during his tough times and they shared a cordial relationship.

He walked till Dr Kashish's clinic where two patients were already waiting. He took a stroll in the hospital's lobby. He didn't understand medicine much, but over time, he had started to feel at home in SVS. He connected with the patients, and he thought about them. He understood humane and the unquestioned belief that the patients had on their doctors. He smiled looking at some of the simple villagers who were happy to take their son back with them. Kushank remembered the kid who had come a month ago, suffering from acute malnutrition and a lot of complications. Seeing him stand on his feet gave Kushank a warm feeling of pride.

Meanwhile, Kushank saw the patients come out of Dr Kashish's clinic. He knocked on the door, "Doctor, May I?"

He stood at the door.

"Since when have we become so formal, Kushank? Please come." Dr Kashish got up to greet him.

Kushank came in and sat down. He smiled and was about to bring the up issue when Dr Kashish explained, "Look, I know there are a few problems that the management has with me. I have in fact, suggested them to cut the losses that they have faced from my monthly salary. Further, I wouldn't like to explain anything else to anyone."

Kushank was left agape. He always knew that this lady was stern, but he also believed in her skills. He asked calmly, "Undoubtedly you aren't answerable to anyone, but, if I asked you as a friend about the matter, will you still not share it with me?"

"Well, I would appreciate your support, but would suggest that you please stay out of it. I wouldn't…"

Kushank insisted, "Kashish, I know if you have put forward a stand, it must be logical. Tell me, I insist."

Dr Kashish saw the honesty in his eyes and explained, "Well, a week ago, a couple had come to me. They suffered a bus accident and unfortunately, the lady had a miscarriage. The couple was not from a well to do family, but their bond was precious. Trust me Kushank,

I have seen marriages break because of infertility, but I was proud to see the husband so supportive of his wife even when she couldn't become a mother. He was honestly happy that we could save his wife. He didn't disown her for the fact that she couldn't bear a child any longer. He wasn't even a graduate and they belonged to a simple background, but the way he handled his wife, I was touched. And then, while they left my clinic with the bill, I heard them talk about their financial crisis. They were in grave need of money, so I asked them to leave the bill slip and go. Since then, the hospital staff had been questioning me about the action…"

Kushank heard her without a blink and saw the spark which Kashish had in her eyes. She was bent on helping the couple. She continued, "I know I became emotional while dealing with my patients and we are not supposed to do that, but at that moment, I couldn't have done anything else for them. I have called them for a few tests too and I'd like to take care of all the expenses of her treatment. I have consulted a foreign hospital and would like to work in collaboration with them."

Kushank smiled.

"I am so sorry. I just keep blabbering."

"No, Kashish, I am sorry. In fact, I would like to support your cause. Figure out the details, we'll help them together. Because, I trust your confidence. Go ahead for the treatment and be rest assured."

Dr Kashish looked up at him and smiled back. She said, "And I thought you were a businessman."

Kushank laughed as he got up to leave. "Well, that I certainly am. The only difference is that here, I am investing in your hope to bring the profit of happiness."

Adding to it, if Kashish was successful, SVS Hospitals could promote their philanthropy. Let's not forget, he was a marketing person too.

It was the first time that Kushank had taken an instant decision. He was much more confident. Thanks to his 'new friend'. The hospital diaries narrated his evolved self.

Dr Kashish looked at him proudly as he walked to his cabin. He was right, all of us are somewhere in the process of learning and as the couple's story says it all, when the bond is real, you don't need to be urbane or rich to express your emotions. The strength of a relationship is measured by the togetherness during the rough patch.

Marriage, isn't just a word. It means togetherness in the face of anything and everything in life.

Crap!

9 p.m.
29 October 2013
College mess, SVS, Bhopal

WELL, THE TITLE OF THE CHAPTER VERY WELL DEFINES THE situation. The situation on the field was just absurd.

Amaira was having her dinner in the mess along with Rajbir, Trisha and Roop and they were talking about their dance practices for Pulse. They were performing a group act and were discussing the costumes and props. A few of the seniors came and joined the group with a wide grin on their faces. Amaira didn't give importance to anyone of them. Though there wasn't a conflict, everyone knew things were not smooth between the seniors and Amaira, especially after she had got Vikrant and Rini expelled. She had ruined their careers and their dreams of becoming doctors. Ego could be curbed for a limited time, but alas! It ends up bringing a tiff between two human beings, and here too, friction was clearly visible.

There was no open tiff, but the cold vibes could easily be felt when the seniors looked at Amaira. As for Amaira, she simply didn't care. For her, only *she* mattered and her friends.

However, while she was mixing her *daal* with the rice, one of her seniors said, "Raj, did you guys check the couple list?"

Raj, pretending to be the clown of the town, said, "No yaar. Who knows better than me what 'singleton' means."

Trisha eyed him with a smug look.

The group laughed. One of Rini's old friend's asked Roop, "And what about you darling? Too busy dating books, eh?"

The seniors loved being sarcastic. Amaira frowned and she got up, "Well I am done. Good night."

Trying to interest Amaira in a conversation was exceptionally tough. Until it was about football or food – or Bollywood – Amaira would be least interested. Grabbing her attention was a wild goose's chase for the seniors. That's when they applied their trump card. One of them said, "Well, Amaira, good night. Just don't forget to check the list on the student's notice board."

They shared notoriously cunning glances.

Amaira walked away. She never liked people with negative vibes. Kabir had always taught her to stay away from such people. But, as she walked out of the mess, Amaira saw a few friends and seniors staring at her. The glances made her feel uncomfortable. One of them commented, "You are a genius, babe."

Amaira felt discomforted and walked in haste. She didn't know the reason behind such looks. She walked briskly, not knowing the reason behind such stares. While walking briskly, her eyes caught her name on the notice board in BOLD CAPITAL LETTERS. And not only was her name on the notice board, there was a collection of photographs attached to it. Amaira walked closer and read the list. The prank was terrible. She had a sweaty forehead as she read. The list read:

'Couple number 1: Kushank sir and our very dear daughter of controversy – Amaira Roy.'

The photographs attached were not passport sized – they were specially 'edited' photographs. They were clicked when Amaira was injured in the gym. Terribly cheap the prank was. Finding herself on the notice board with obscene remarks wasn't something which went very well with her. Character and questions on character are definitely not a small thing. Anger was evidently visible in her eyes.

Till now, every relation in her life was named, but her equation with Kushank had remained unnamed for a long time. Amaira never thought about their friendship otherwise, until that day but whenever she met Kushank, she realized that everything was abrupt yet soothing.

But, whatever their relation was, for Amaira it could never be categorized the way the notice board did. Amaira could now understand why there were uncomfortable glances towards her in the mess. And adding salt to the open wound, a friend came and said, "What a genius you are, chick. I mean getting so close with the trustee. Perhaps, that's why you spent nights away from hostel, eh?"

Amaira walked away. She knew she couldn't shut all the mouths. There was no point in doing so. She even knew that at this point, the mess was buzzing with gossip about her.

She kept a straight face as she walked to her room.

But she felt sick. Dizzy...thinking about the pictures. She was deeply hurt. Yes, she was. She wiped away a drop of anger-filled tear from her eyes as she moved towards the hostel, but just before turning for her hostel, her steps turned towards Kushank's cabin. She went and knocked on the door. Kushank looked up indifferently.

He didn't have the courage to face the world, so he decided to turn away. His love, his admiration, his care had all kneeled down in front of his importance to what people would think and the zeal to escape problems.

And – we thought Kushank had changed?

He turned away, leaving Amaira in a miserable condition. She felt betrayed as a friend. She never thought about having feelings for him, but he couldn't even respect her emotions. Amaira walked back angrily, tears flowing from her hazel eyes.

On the other hand, Kushank too had tears of guilt in his eyes which though didn't spill, but tortured him deep inside. He knew he was wrong and unjust, and he was being a coward, but being strong demanded strength – mental strength. He also knew that he couldn't challenge conventions. His college's reputation, his chair, the taste of power which he had started to enjoy was all at stake because of his friendship with Amaira. For him, that moment demanded him to choose between his love and the eyes of the world.

Needless to say, he chose the latter.

Amaira went inside her room and locked herself. Yes, Kushank's ignorance made her weaker. She thought until then that whatever would come, Kushank was one person she could turn to. Amaira always knew that her personality didn't need anyone, didn't depend on anyone for happiness but on herself. But Kushank was supposedly a friend? And friends were supposed to be supportive?

The seniors were happy to see their junior suffer. Little did they know that it was she who believed in making people suffer. It was just at that moment when a drop of tear fell on her lap that her conscience woke her up.

'Since when has Amaira Roy started being affected by such morons,' she asked herself.

'Cowards cry over split milk Amu, get up and show the world what being Amaira is,' the voice insisted.

Amaira sat on her bed and thought about everything and everyone – the shallow seniors, the gossiping batch-mates, and the trustee of her college. Nobody stood by her but she had to stand by herself. She wiped every teardrop, and with the tears, she wiped away those fake relations which had played a key role in hurting her. She knew she could re-assemble herself. She knew she could be the Amaira that she always was.

Sweet bitterness would be the exact word.

She knew her strengths by now, and her weaknesses too!

❖

As for Kushank, he was dejected and alone. Amaira at least had herself, Kushank couldn't even console himself by saying he had himself. He was all alone. His under-confidence was drowning him yet again. Even then he couldn't stand up for what was right. *Could nervousness and fear destroy someone? Could it? I never knew.*

At that moment, he thought about facing the board members regarding the controversy and pictures. The senior doctors had called for an urgent meeting and knowing them well, Kushank knew he would have a tough time. He also knew that Amaira would have to face a lot. He was aware of everything yet he turned his eyes away from reality. He had feelings, but had no strength to stand by them.

He signed in to his laptop to find an escape from reality, but was dumbstruck by reading the comments on the confession page of SVS:

'This chick is too hot. One moment she is seen helping the trustee and the next she is his girlfriend.

PS: Babe, I own two crores too. (Who knows I am next?)'

Another cheap thread was:

'Amaira Roy. We just thought she was different. The same old story! I smell a Bollywood movie. Money, haan?'

Kushank felt weak in his knees when he read all these comments. For once, he wanted to shout at every freaking person who was insulting and humiliating a person close to his heart. But, what would that do? It would just worsen the situation. He knew his mom had also heard about the rumour and Kushank, who had always stayed away from home, didn't know how Mrs Khanna would react. He couldn't gather the courage to meet his mother as well.

Meanwhile, the clips which he had been storing in his mind's storage device started to play, just that this time, the ambience was sombre. Kushank knew Amaira had a special place in his life, but what should be the name given to that place? A friend? Was it the answer, Kushank wondered. However, just when he was busy fiddling with his mobile phone, his mother came into his room. Kushank got up and sat next to her.

"Kush, why are you so worried?"

"Maa, those photographs are edited. I was with Amaira at the gym, but she had slipped from the treadmill and I was just helping her as a…"

He stammered. And it is a fact known worldwide that mothers are the best judges when it comes to their kids. Mrs Khanna interrupted him and explained, "Look Kush, first find answers to your doubts, then try to put forward your views. And what I come to know is that the college is not speaking much about you, but about the girl. Now, I just want you to handle this maturely. Your actions would in a way affect the young girl. Act maturely and don't be a coward."

Amaira was popular. Mrs Khanna had heard Dr Raghuvanshi crib about how Amaira was, she had heard her staff talk and whisper about the girl and she knew Amaira was an agent of change. She had, in fact, made everyone rethink about them in the ragging episode. However, the mother knew that her son had, yet again, decided to take the easier way out. *She knew Kush inside out.* She shook her head in despair and moved away. Distanced would be the word.

Kushank thought, perhaps over-thought about the situation. He knew there had to be some corrective measure taken. We are human and we know blaming someone else is not as difficult as it is to stand with the accused and face everything. And once that patch has passed, relationships take just a magical turn. However, for Kushank the facts were problematic. The list had somewhere expressed what his unconscious mind had always been thinking of! But, he lacked courage to accept it. Now, in the middle of the confusion, Amaira and Kushank had to deal with the muddle of gossip – together or as singletons.

❖

Next morning, the sun brought with it a new spirit in Amaira. She got up knowing the fact that college was going to be tough, but at the same time, she was confident of shutting the blabbering mouths. She knew she wasn't wrong, she knew she wasn't dating Kushank and she knew that the photographs were edited. The information was enough for Amaira to be on her front foot.

Amaira was back.

She got up and got ready in a beige crop top and denim shorts. She kept her notebooks and was just about to leave when her mind, for a second took a leap into a world she didn't want to enter into at that time. Yes, she thought about Kushank and the way he had behaved. Amaira frankly didn't want to talk to him. In a fraction of that second, she knew Kush had stepped back when she stood outside his cabin. Drenched in embarrassment, Amaira for the first time expected someone to take a stand for her and shut all the questioning mouths. She expected her friend to stand by her. Biggest mistake, she thought. That perhaps was the only little minute that broke her emotionally. She felt vulnerable and needed a friend whom she had always supported. Kushank had, from his denying eyes, taken away every right of being her friend.

She wondered for a moment about herself and Kushank, but very quickly her brain stepped ahead and she came back to practicalities.

She casually took her bag and ran down the staircase as she made her way to the classroom. She moved ahead confidently and didn't bother to even look at people around her. She, for a moment had thought she needed Kushank, but she needed no one at all.

They didn't even deserve her silence. This was Amaira.

But Kushank wasn't Amaira, and that was the biggest drawback he had. In his cabin, Dr Bose, the Dean sat right in front of him. He said with a taut face, "This happens when young lads like you are given such power. Kushank sir, I require an answer. This college works on some principles. And you are certainly a threat…"

He continued. Kushank was nervous, but he knew handling Mr Bose wasn't going to be that tough. He replied, even more sternly. This was the exact way in which he kept control over his staff – hitting them on their weaknesses.

"Sir, what about the ragging? I wonder how you missed that on your part?"

Mr Bose was quiet. Silence followed until Mr Kumar walked in and added oil into the burning fire. He started lecturing Kushank on how he should have taken care of the protocols and rules of the college. The two middle-aged men started to impart all the knowledge that they had about morals. Discipline was the key word. I wonder where did all this go when they were tolerating ragging? Anyhow. Yes, Kushank felt irritated and just to stop the lecture, Kushank exclaimed, "I don't need to give answers for a mere student. I am the trustee and every girl wants to link her name with me. So, should I answer for everyone's dreams? Let the youngster keep dreaming. I am certainly much above the age. I don't find this an issue to discuss. You may leave."

Unluckily for him, his excuse was overheard by Amaira, who was passing by his cabin. Hatred was the word now. She walked confidently, but the few words managed to give her a shocking reality check. 'Could she be so wrong in judging someone?' she questioned herself.

She was deeply affected by each and every word he had said, yet again. Her ambiguous feelings would have never made her weak, but Kushank's words had. She hadn't befriended him because he was the trustee of SVS; she didn't have dicey feelings for him because he was powerful, and she didn't even think about money – she didn't need to. But, the mere fact that he thought she was someone who would befriend him for money, and someone who would create all this drama for attention was unbelievable.

Was it all he learnt about her in these days? She was so mad that she took the flower vase kept in the corner of the corridor and threw it right in front of Kushank's cabin.

He ran to check the sound and saw a ferocious Amaira in front of him. She didn't speak a single word; she didn't complain, but just fumed with anger, perhaps not at Kushank but at herself. Most certainly, Kushank had said everything to fix the situation easily. He was scared and he took a decision which he knew was wrong. He wanted an easy way out. However, when he saw Amaira, he knew he had invited trouble. Amaira, on the other hand, stood firm to the ground, speaking a thousand words through her angry eyes. Every bit of that silence shattered Kushank. He might not have had the guts to explain himself, but his feelings were honest and true.

He knew Amaira was particular about trust and that had certainly been shattered. He tried to walk towards her and Amaira threw another glass vase on the floor. She turned around and began walking towards her class, stepping on the broken pieces of glass. It was their broken bond which she had moved away from.

She walked away angrily towards the classroom and attended the lecture on anatomy. Looking at the fury which poured from her eyes, nobody, literally nobody, including Rajbir tried to talk to her. Poor Arjun, he hadn't analyzed the weather and made his mind to talk to Amaira after the class. Amaira, who looked petrifying, replied arrogantly, "Arjun, stop all your nonsense. I know you aren't guilty of what you did. So, stop being a puppy and following me. Get lost now."

But while she was talking, another classmate, who apparently didn't like Amaira much, commented "Amaira, why are you venting your anger on Arjun? Truth…"

She was still speaking when Amaira grabbed her wrist and held it tightly. The girl shrieked in pain. Amaira shouted loudly,

"You were saying something. Say. *Say!*"

The girl yelped in anguish. Her wrist was aching. Amaira continued, "Call me a goon from now. And trust me, if it had been real, I would have accepted my relationship long back. Editing photos and clipping them on the notice board is nothing but cowardice. I don't care and I don't know anything about that man except for the fact that he is the owner of the college where fortunately or unfortunately I am studying. Get that straight. And if at all my ears hear any stupid rumor, I'll teach you how to talk. Class, learn to talk in whispers now because sweetness has caused me disastrous diabetes. Bitter is the new sweet from now on."

That poor girl suffered all the anger which Amaira wanted to vent on the situation. Kushank, who was passing by, walked inside the class. He walked to the classroom and heard everything clearly. Somewhere deep in his heart, he was hurt.

He had decided to make a call to Amaira and clarify everything, but he heard Amaira make herself crystal clear. In fact, it was expected from her, he thought. Amaira was, after all, an independent and overtly frank girl. Kushank didn't have anything else to say. He had received all the answers. He too felt a silent anguish inside his heart, but covered it with his sophistication. He gathered himself for once and walked inside the classroom, looking at the fuming lady. He went in and looked at Amaira with sorrowful eyes.

How he wished she understood him.

How much he wanted to erase what he had heard a moment ago and how much she craved to delete the dialogue she heard.

Kushank said to Amaira, politely, disguising his anguish by humbleness, "This is a college. I would suggest that everybody maintains its dignity. Please maintain discipline inside the campus and trust me guys, I'll not be polite the next time."

Amaira replied with stern expressions, "Sorry sir. I'd make sure discipline is not compromised."

And she moved away. Every single word which she had spoken was accompanied by anger and an unknown frustration. Apparently, even she didn't know what was going on in her mind but she knew whatever it was, it wasn't good. She wanted Kushank to make things clear; that's what Kushank wanted too. But the situation had worsened instead. Perhaps they didn't know what they wanted, but were in the race to pretend, and pretense, my friend, has never brought about any good.

Amaira walked away and Kushank was left thinking about everything. His mom was right, he still had to find answers to a lot of unanswered questions. Amaira had, once and for all, closed the chapter.

It's the world of the instant

1:45 a.m.
23 October 2013
Terrace, SVS, Bhopal

THE DAY WAS HARD, HARSH AND HECTIC FOR AMAIRA. SHE sat in the most deserted of all places, finding solace for herself in her own company. She just sat, cutting herself away from all human communication. Little did she know that friends at times could be irritating. Kratika and Karan came looking for her and once they spotted her, they came and sat with her.

Before they could say anything, Amaira firmly requested, "Leave me alone for some time. I love you both, but just let me be."

They wouldn't. Kratika said, "We will. But you tell us, how will we win day after tomorrow if we won't practice for Pulse? We need you to come along and practice with us."

Amaira frowned. She knew this was a ploy to take her with them. She replied arrogantly, "I remember my steps. You guys practice."

Karan intervened and said, "And what about your bag, Amaira? Packed? We are leaving tomorrow morning, darling."

Amaira all of a sudden remembered about her tickets. She exclaimed, "What the— damn! I haven't packed anything. How

167

am I to flaunt my dresses in the fest? Let's go and get ready to check out some hot guys, Kratika. Delhi, here we come!"

❖

12:45 p.m.
25 October 2013
AIIMS Auditorium, Delhi

"Where on earth is Rajbir, Trisha?"

Amaira asked, dressed in a white blouse and white knee length skirt, all set for the dance competition at Pulse. The group arrived and were geared up to rock their contemporary act, but just before the competition was about to begin, Rajbir vanished.

How very dramatic, don't we want to say?

Whatever it was, Amaira asked her group to stay as she rushed in the direction of the hostel rooms. Rajbir, the Mr X for the moment, had even left his phone with Trisha. There was no way to find him except to run around and AIIMS, my friend, is such a big campus that it's impossible to trace someone. After all, almost all medical colleges had their teams there.

As Amaira ran towards the food court, looking here and there, she bumped into an unknown face. But, the 'accident' resulted in a disaster. The coke, which the guy was carrying, splashed on Amaira's white blouse. She shouted, slowly looking up, "Walking in a garden or what?"

As she looked up, she saw a face which was innocently honest. The subtle, yet dashing hot looks were what struck her first. And then her eyes caught sight of his well-toned body, which was peeping from his partially unbuttoned shirt. Yet, Amaira as she was cribbed, "How am I to dance now? You ruined it all. Leave now!"

All this while, the guy looked at Amaira with a dreamy expression. She looked so beautiful in white with her hair slyly waving around her face. *Amaira was fond of movies, bollywood movies. Wasn't she?*

He said in the softest voice, "I am – I am really sorry. Trust me, I just looked away for a moment."

Amaira, in the meantime saw Rajbir passing by her. She shouted, "Raj. Damn-it. Don't you know you should be backstage? As it is the DU colleges are really good. Look…" she pointed at her dress and the coke which had started to make a stain over it and continued,

"My dress is ruined. All thanks to you."

She looked at the guy.

Rajbir looked at him with an apologetic expression as the guy observed Amaira. He proposed, "I think I could help you. Come with me."

For the first time, Amaira didn't say anything. His honesty had made an impression on her. He held her wrist and walked briskly towards the painting area. There, he quickly sprayed white colour over her dress and lo! It looked whiter than before. (*I all of a sudden am reminded of those washing powder ads, aren't you?*)

Amaira looked at him with surprise. She smiled broadly. She looked beautiful when she smiled, he thought. He smiled back. Amaira's heart skipped a heartbeat for the first time in her life. She started turning towards the auditorium, when he said politely, "Thank you for me is always over a coffee."

Amaira smirked and replied, "I just thought you are different. But…let's meet after my performance."

He smiled. Every time he smiled, Amaira loved his innocence. He asked as she walked away, "How am I to find you?"

Amaira's reply was Amaira-ish, "People try hard to find happiness. You can't even try to find me?"

She grinned and ran away, without turning back. On the other hand, a girl tapped him on his shoulders and he went happily with her, definitely with his thoughts around the new girl he had just met.

❖

The dance was a hit. There were several moments when Amaira just thought she would lose her balance or Trisha would miss the lift, but nothing happened. Everything went on smoothly. The crowd went gaga over their performance and most of the audience grooved with them, even on the slow tracks that they performed. Amaira was exceptionally elated with the limelight she received.

Kabir's sister she was, after all!

She happily grabbed the attention and as she was gathering her props and planning to join her friends, the boy she had met in the morning held her wrist and took her along, outside the hall. Amaira, who by now would have murdered someone for doing something of this kind, said sternly, "What's all this?"

The boy, who looked uncomfortable, replied in his ever so soft voice, "I knew you wouldn't come otherwise."

Absolutely correct. Amaira would have even forgotten their meeting that morning. She smiled, unlike herself. Perhaps it was attraction.

Was it?

Both of them walked till the coffee counter in the huge food zone and bought two coffees. Amaira paid for hers. And while walking back to their hostels, both of them realised that they were inevitably attracted to each other. In fact, he did confess that he liked her carefree nature, but he was already committed to someone for eight-and-a-half years now. Amaira loved his honestly and loyalty towards his relationship.

They had spent just an hour together; they hadn't even exchanged names. He had just heard people calling her 'Amaira'.

They didn't even know their whereabouts, destinations, ways, or probably we are over thinking; feelings don't need any such material information. Amaira, shell shocked by the information, stammered for words. She was both impressed by his love for his girlfriend and somewhere disappointed with the expression of love. She was attracted to him, but love and the like was never her cup of tea.

That we know! Don't we?

She just looked at him. His honest eyes forbade him from lying, she knew. She gave him a friendly, tight hug. She said as they parted, "You'd be one character of my story that I'll not forget. And trust me, your girlfriend is a happy, young lady. Be happy. In fact, if I really believed in love and all, I would have fallen for you. But fortunately for you, life is happier for me enjoying my singlehood!"

As they parted, she smiled. He smiled back. Everything was so instant that he just didn't know what had happened. Perhaps, love had blindfolded him. And the best part about him was that he believed in keeping the faith of someone in his life. That was something which fascinated Amaira a lot. She was sure her thoughts would be webbed around that face for some time. As for him, his girl came towards him and they walked hand in hand, off to explore the capital city of Delhi. Romance and love had to follow!

Instant feelings, instant emotions but permanent memories – there was a lot more happening at Pulse! Every night was a big party with DJs, music, and food – what else does one need to have a happy life! Certainly, Amaira and the gang enjoyed every bit of the trip. Late at night, Amaira did think about the boy before sleep lay heavy on her eyes.

Lessons life learns

12.40 a.m.
25 October 2015
Kushank's Cabin, SVS, Bhopal

WHERE, ON THE ONE HAND, AMAIRA WAS ENJOYING HERSELF with her friends and letting her hair down, Kushank had started to enter the web of guilt, self-consciousness and depression. He was building this web around himself – all by himself. The thought of losing a friend – a girl who meant more than a friend – was eating his mind like a termite. He wanted to talk to her, but she wouldn't listen, he wanted to make her understand, but the situation would't allow her to see reason.

The problem was that Kushank's love was true, but his personality was again and again creating obstacles in his path of happiness. He felt helpless.

After Amaira left for Delhi, Kushank started to feel the void around him, and uncertainty, doubts, despair and depression started to crawl from his feet to his head, silently building a web around his body. He sat at the same table from where he had started to work at SVS. He thought about himself and his journey. He knew that he had pushed himself to work harder only because of one reason – Amaira.

And there was no point repeating what he had done. He was torn to pieces which he tried to gather, but didn't have the courage to. Amaira was his motivation, and his inspiration. She was the one who was like a backbone for him. He was getting lost in the ocean of disappointment. At that moment, Vishesh called him and informed him about the crisis at their workplace.

"The game that we launched is a disaster. It's taking much more space than expected and the user reviews are pathetic. The investors are on our head. We need you here, Kushank."

Kushank heard every word unambitiously and kept the phone down. Ambition had left his life alongside Amaira's departure. Nothing mattered to him now. He had lost Amaira, the only hope which could keep him going. And just when he started to sign some budget reports, regardless of the mistakes, Mr Kumar entered with some challenging news.

"Sir, a complaint has been registered against our hospital today."

Kushank inquired about the case and heard everything. It was an influential businessman who had decided to sue the hospital, holding them responsible for the death of his relative. Powerful meant the proceedings were swift. The lawyer had already issued a notice in the name of Kushank. Kushank asked, "Who was the doctor involved? And are we at fault?"

"Dr Das. No, we are certainly not at fault, sir. There were complications and the damage was irreparable."

Kushank was no longer worried; he had lost the battle beforehand. He knew he wouldn't be able to fight.

"Ask our lawyer to revert, asking them about any compromise which the party expects from us. That's all we can do."

Mr Kumar, baffled with the decision, replied hastily, "But sir, we have a stronger case. The reports suggest that we are not at fault. Then why should we compromise? It will make their case stronger and if at all they don't agree to a compromise, we'll have to make rounds of the court."

Kushank didn't listen.

"Even if we fight the case, we won't win it."

Pessimism is the worst enemy of ambition and dream.

Once it starts to build a wall around you, you'll land being a human who is alive yet without any oxygen of hope. It's the worst one could expect from life. Isn't it?

He had given up on everything. Mr Kumar, dejected, left the cabin and called a meeting with their lawyer. It was like one movie which had a bumpy start and then everything started to look better. Kushank had of late started to look brighter and hopeful, and then, all of a sudden, everything started to fall apart. The climax perhaps started to run anti-clockwise. Kushank was starting to become what he was before Amaira, or perhaps, worse than that.

Mr Kumar kept Mrs Khanna in the loop and told her about Kushank's decisions. Mrs Khanna, aware of the turmoil which had swept Kushank's confidence, replied, "Definitely not. I will tell you how to handle this case. Send the lawyer to my cabin. Kushank is insane. It's not as if we are facing such a case for the first time."

The mother, who had been filled with pride for her son, could see the house of cards falling piece by piece. She knew about Kushank's business too. Vishesh had told her about the failure of their new app and this time, Kushank neither had a hand to hold his and say that he was capable, nor did he have his inspiration to keep him going. He knew he wouldn't be able to manage anything.

Perhaps, he knew too much, eh?

In the next three days, he took the last decision about his business. He called Vishesh and declared, "I am quitting our business. You can use my investment to save the business."

Vishesh was shocked. He needed money to save his firm, but he also needed his friend in the long run. Kushank had decided to give up on everything he loved. He had accepted defeat in everything he was doing or would do in the future. He had already accepted that nothing would work. That's why they say, dependency kills the hope of individuality. Kushank was so miserably desperate for a partner who would motivate him that when he was left alone, or say when he chose to be alone, he couldn't tolerate the void around him. The emptiness broke him. He left his dream half-lived and the regret of not being able to stand by his love started to spread like poison in his mind. All this while, Amaira was away and in the little span that he spent without seeing her, talking to her or thinking about her made him more and more vulnerable. Darkness was all that he could identify with. The person that he had been was back – under-confident, cowardly and unable to take a stand.

Amaira was enjoying the heat of Pulse. Apart from the events at the fest, her friends forced her to join them on their sightseeing trips, even though she had been to those places many times. It was the ninth time that she was visiting the water show at Akshardham Temple.

Rajbir and Trisha, the most amiable couple, walked through the gardens of Akshardham hand in hand. Amaira literally loved them. Both of them complemented one another so well. They walked cutely as Amaira walked around alone and checked out some new dishes in the canteen.

She grabbed a bite, and then, as the whole group ran to get seats for the water show, Amaira squeezed in too. Kratika, Karan and Roop accompanied her. The lovely lights, the attention-grabbing music and the didactic tale that the fountains narrated was exceptional. Amaira loved every bit of it.

After the show, she bid farewell to her group, that was to stay in Delhi for another five days, while she was going back to Bhopal. She wanted to relax a bit before the terminals started. She was going to take a three-day break at home, where all she wanted was to chill, have some good junk food and watch as many movies as she could. She also wanted to spend some time with Kabir. Kabir was busy with either Suhani's Mumbai preparations or gathering sponsors for the annual fest at SSRC. Amaira wanted to talk endlessly with her only true best friend. She wanted to share everything that had happened with Kushank.

So she took the metro home. She was all set to surprise him.

Who knew, instead she would have one of the most pleasant surprises.

As Amaira rang the bell, twice, thrice and infinite times as she always did, Suhani came running from the kitchen, with flour stuck to her hands and an apron around her waist. Unknowing of anything, Suhani opened the door. Amaira, who expected Kabir to be home by this hour, looked strangely at the new face that she saw in her house with suspicion in her eyes. Kabir had hidden Suhani's truth from Amaira and his parents. Probably he was unsure of their reactions. Unfortunately for him, Amaira was home while he was struggling with some budgeting in the union room. Suhani looked baffled; she didn't know how to react. Amaira, on the other hand, looked at her with suspicious eyes and commented, "Has Ramesh left the job?"

Suhani looked blank. Amaira played with her eyebrows and just in the way which the detectives inquire, she asked, *Over dramatic, wasn't she?* "Are you the new cook?"

Suhani shook her head. She looked down meekly. By this time, Amaira walked to the guest room and saw some 'lovely' pictures on

Suhani's desk. Happy and romantic pictures of Kabir and herself. Amaira realized who Suhani was. She smiled and then, thought of having some fun. She pestered Suhani with questions and did not let her breathe until she told her every little detail. Suhani, just like an innocent kid, narrated the whole story bit by bit, until Kabir rang the bell. Amaira ran and banged into him. She gave him a tight hug. She was proud of him for what he had done for Suhani.

Kabir, who had just had some lame arguments in the union room, was shocked to see her. He looked at Suhani who reassured him through her eyes. Kabir found solace in those eyes. Amaira observed the eye contact and smiled.

Though she would never agree, but she liked love stories.

As the excitement came down, the trio had a sumptuous dinner. Suhani was an excellent cook. Amaira, licking her fingers said, "Suhani, I don't know why this man didn't tell me about you. Had I known you cook so well, I would have happily stayed with you, Bhabhiji."

Bhabhiji? Kabir's ears went up in shock. He frowned at Amaira. She smirked and didn't miss a chance to pull his leg. That was mandatory.

Sibling love, uh!

Over some crispy nachos, they discussed their entangled, yet beautiful lives, sitting cross-legged on the bed. Amaira had already told them everything about Kushank. Suhani did feel that at some points Amaira had been impulsive, but she knew, saying anything wouldn't change her.

Nothing could change her.

Kabir, on the other hand, talked about the events which he was handling. At the same time, while he was talking, Suhani interrupted, "Also, Kabir is madly into politics these days, Amaira."

A note of complaint was clearly noticable in her voice. Amaira looked at Kabir and then made her point, "He's always been into politics, Suhani."

"Certainly. But, being desperate for the ticket is incorrect, right?" Suhani pleaded. Kabir looked annoyed with the way in which Suhani kept cribbing about his political ambitions. He said, looking at Suhani, in a stern voice, "People have some goals in life. And it is said, everything is fair in love and war – and everything is fairer in ambition."

Suhani seemed distressed. This wasn't new, though. *Relations don't just work on love, there are moments of stress, there are moments of arguments that can affect momentarily but at the end, the bigger the fight, the closer you get to your partner.*

She didn't say much but got up and walked out of the room, greeting Amaira with a warm hug. "Good night dear. I am a little sleepy. You guys carry on."

Amaira went back to sit with Kabir.

"Kabir, I have seen you ambitious. But today, your eyes had negative ambitions. What's all this? Since when have we become so distant that you can't share such important things of your life with me? You trust me, don't you?"

Kabir, fiddling with his mobile phone, preferred staying mum. Amaira, in anger snatched his mobile and threw it away. He snarled, "Amaira! What the—"

Amaira interrupted him sharply.

"What's going on with you Kabir? You know you are deserving."

Kabir replied, irritated by both the women in his life, "Deserving is never enough. You need contacts, money and muscle power. And you will not understand that, little one, be happy with your little victories."

Amaira wasn't very happy with the way in which Kabir was behaving. Perhaps, it was just a bad day he was having. Still, she explained, "Fine. You are correct and Suhani isn't. Point accepted. But, just before going to bed tonight, think of what you really, like really wanted in life. Was it the centre stage? (*Yes, it was*), or was it blind ambition? Ambition is one word even I am passionately in love with, but our eyes are with us to judge the paths. It's all upon you. Good night, bhai!"

She got up and as she wore her slippers she said, "I am going to meet Sharad tomorrow. He just recovered from a bad accident. Just thought would tell you. "

She walked a step ahead and turned back once again to say, "And, before I leave, I hope you remember that the girl whom you have been so rude to is leaving the city day after tomorrow."

Every word which Amaira said before the last bit seemed like bullets for Kabir. He knew that he wasn't the person that he was becoming. He was the one madly in love with Suhani and that day, her suggestions became irksome. He was always capable, but the influence was making him forget his capabilities and think about alternative ways. He sat back all through the night and thought about what Amaira had said. He sat on this thinking chair and thought and thought until he knew what path he had to take.

Suhani had locked the room and was busy packing her stuff for Mumbai, packing almost all her memories that she had gathered in the house. She was arranging some of her dresses when she, amidst the cool flowing breeze which brushed her face, thought about every moment with Kabir.

Was the argument worth it, she wondered. She knew she wouldn't trust herself if he didn't teach her to do so. He had built a new confidence in her and every memory which she was packing in the black suitcase urged her to get up and talk to him – to share his confusions, ambiguities and aims.

Suhani got up, opened the door and walked straight into Kabir's room. Kabir, still thinking in the dark, didn't notice her coming. It was when she stood firmly in front of him that he realized that she was there. She kept her palm on his and in a reassuring voice, said, "Kabir, I am sorry. I know I have become a nagging girlfriend."

Kabir, who in the past two hours had realized every wrong step that he was willing to take, said, with tears in his eyes, "No, I know I was too unlike Kabir Roy. I had every power in the union, yet I wanted more. Power definitely is addictive. You know Suhani, I still want power because I know I deserve it. I will, I know, but through correct means."

Suhani smiled. She gave him a tight hug. Definitely power was addictive, but there are always ways to reach your goal.

He said, still holding her tightly in his arms, "No matter where I go, your affection brings me back; no matter how far I fly, your simplicity keeps me grounded; no matter what I do, I'll end up falling for you."

I am glad Kabir chose the right path.

Amaira, who was wide awake, shouted from the living room, "Guys, don't forget there's a kid in the house. Close the door if you want to!"

She smirked, as she peeped into the room. Kabir and Suhani parted awkwardly. Amaira smirked and gave her brother a tight hug. After which she just yawned and said, "Enough for the day. Happys endings."

Was it the ending, I wonder? It was a start to a brand new bond that just knitted two hearts together. Long distance, whatsoever people wonder about it, stays fresh and close to my heart. It might have a distance, but the distance works for diminishing the real 'distance' between people. You might talk less, but when you talk, your content is unmatchable; you might see each other less, but when you finally meet, there is an altogether new ambience. You might spend less quality time, but whatever little you get to spend is enough to face the challenges that life throws at you for the next session.

Cutting the long lecture on long distance short, there was a brand new bond and a brand new phase in Suhani's life. She had won half the battle and rest was waiting to be achieved.

Confidence is the word.

Live to live a life
which can save a life

12 p.m.
26 October 2015
Templeton Estate, DLF, Gurgaon

GURGAON, AS I KEEP SAYING, IS THE CITY OF SKY SCRAPERS. Tall, huge and magnificent buildings which are competing with the sky to touch the stars. It was amidst such buildings that Sharad lived. Sharad, if you remember was one of Amaira's classmates. Amaira was a true friend. She might not stand and celebrate the happy cheers, but would make it a point to be there in times of need. She took an auto and reached the society where Sharad lived. As she reached the building and was waiting for the lift to come down, a lady joined her. With an infant as pink as the flowers in her arms, the mother took full care of her child, protecting him from every possible thing that she could. Wrapped in his mother's arms, the child looked so terribly cute. Amaira instantly connected with the little kid.

She smiled at him and made kiddish gestures with her fingers to grab his attention. The child did respond.

Children are real jokers. Why, you ask? Because, we love jokers, I say!

The lift finally arrived after waiting for a couple of more minutes. As the lift stopped at the ground floor, Amaira first held the doors by her palm, making sure that the infant and his mother were safely inside, after which, she got in and pressed the button which read 21. Sharad lived in the sky, she marked. As they moved inside, the lady smiled at her kid who was making cute faces. He was definitely a very happy child. and secretly, I am in love with happy children. Plus, the bond is instant. The lady too resided on the twenty-first floor.

Amaira asked the lady, a sweet urbane mother, "Your kid is too cute. What's his name?"

"Madhav," she answered with a smile.

The lift was suffocating. In a few moments, there were more than thirteen people in the small lift and soon, even with the little fan working, Amaira started sweating. There were so many people and it became difficult to breathe. The child, who had looked happy and cheerful a moment ago, started getting cranky. The mother kept fanning him with her hands and tried making him comfortable.

When the overcrowded lift moved upwards after the sixth floor, it stopped midway. Amaira was terribly scared of lifts. She preferred climbing ten floors rather than taking the lift when she was alone. Right now, she was shivering. There were ten odd people in the lift and it had been a minute since the lift had stopped. It was getting suffocating inside. Madhav, the little kid too started weeping loudly. His mother looked worried. Amaira, gulping all her fear moved till the door and shouted along with the other people. But the guards were helpless as there was a technical breakdown and they weren't able to fix it. They had asked the company to send a team as soon as possible. But, in the next two minutes, everyone inside started feeling anxious. As Amaira stood near the door, she heard the mother shouting, "Madhav – what happened, baba?"

Amaira and nine other pairs of eyes turned instantly towards the infant. His mother was crying. Amaira rushed towards her and asked what was wrong. The lady had become hysterical and couldn't say anything. Amaira, who was terribly scared herself, tried to push aside her fear for the moment.

She took the infant in her arms and checked his pulse. She was shocked to find that Madhav wasn't breathing.

Her hands froze, her eyes had tears and her heart was thudding at an unbelievable speed. Amaira almost broke down, but realized she couldn't. She remembered Raghuvanshi sir's classes on emergencies. She asked everyone to make some space. By now, even the adults were feeling breathless. The mother was crying uncontrollably.

Amaira looked around her and felt pressure building up in her mind. She felt weak in her knees but she knew she couldn't – she couldn't afford to lose a single moment. She was claustrophobic and the building suffocation was haunting her terribly. She remembered how she used to hold on to her parents during any crisis. But, that day, she saw a little infant who had been blissfully cheerful moments ago, now lying breathless.

I have to do something. I have to forget my fear and save Madhav.

The other people in the lift kept suggesting ideas, but no one touched the child. Amaira recalled what Raghuvanshi sir always said, *"Be calm when everyone else is panicky."*

Amaira held Madhav, placed him on the floor and checked his respiration. He wasn't breathing. This fact gave her chills but she stayed calm.

'He isn't breathing, what should I do?'

'Sir said CPR is what helps in such conditions.'

'CPR, let me rethink. Yes, CPR.'

She performed an immediate CPR on the infant.

She had decided not to give up.

She pressed his chest with two of her fingers and gave thirty compressions continuously and gave him two breaths through the mouth. She kept repeating it again and again. By this time, the lift had stopped at the seventh floor. Amaira picked up the kid and ran outside. She knew his mother was in no condition to handle him and at that moment; Amaira had to act strong.

Emotions at times make us weak. And they can help us grow stronger too. Amaira used them for strength. She had to save Madhav.

She quickly continued the compression and breaths in the ratio of 30:2. She shouted and asked someone to call the ambulance as she kept performing the CPR on Madhav. There was an unknown connection with him.

Amaira was miserably scared. She was shivering inside, but she knew she couldn't let her fear come between her duty and her patient.

She continued the compressions persistently and during her efforts, she heard a faint sound of a breath. It seemed magical, heavenly to be precise. The breath that we take for granted was immeasurable in that moment. It was after seven or eight rounds of compressions that the child had responded. He was alive!

The mother, who herself was in a very vulnerable condition ran as she saw her child's movement. She saw his little fingers moving. Madhav was alive and he had started breathing again. His eyes were open; his organs were working.

Amaira, who couldn't believe for once that she had saved a life, didn't lose her calm. She knew Madhav needed medical support. She asked the mother to accompany her as she ran down the stairs, holding the child tightly. Amaira asked the lady to drive to the hospital as fast as she could.

"Break a few signals, I don't care. Just keep driving," Amaira instructed.

In the meanwhile, Madhav had regained consciousness. He was happily back to life. As Amaira held him carefully in her arms, the lady drove to the nearest hospital where they got Madhav checked and were relaxed to find that all his organs were working normally. The doctors appreciated Amaira's efforts, but that appreciation was nothing in front of the smile that lit up the child's face.

It was this nano-moment in which Amaira realized the goals of her life. They suddenly became crystal clear. She realized what being a doctor meant; she realized what saving a life meant; and most importantly, she realized what she meant to herself. She had, in that millisecond decided to become the best cardiologist of the country. Madhav was the sole reason why Amaira's aim became so clear in front of her eyes.

The mother's gratitude and Madhav's innocence took all her affection. Madhav's mother hugged Amaira tightly.

"You saved my child. You are an angel."

She wasn't an angel; she was a doctor.

Amaira couldn't stop her tears in that moment. She hugged the little child and with every breath that she could feel him taking, she reassured herself of his well being. She smiled and handed over Madhav to his mother and ran towards the terrace of the hospital, where she shouted loudly.

She vented out the pressure that had built inside her. In that minute, she had vented out everything which stopped her from achieving her dreams. From that moment onwards, the sole reason for her existence was to become the best cardiologist of the country and save more lives. And being the stubborn person that she was, she was sure she would achieve it.

Her motto was clear since always to never stop, but the destination became more clearly visible that day.

That's why I say, *sabbaticals are beneficial, even if they last for a single moment.*

Epilogue

AMAIRA, KUSHANK, SUHANI AND KABIR ARE LIKE MY FRIENDS now. But there were questions I wanted my storyteller to answer. I asked, looking towards the scenic beauty of the mountains, turning to the girl who narrated the whole story to me, "But, didn't Amaira have feelings for Kushank? Did she not like him? And Suhani…did she achieve her goals? And most importantly, who are you? How do you know the story?"

As I kept asking questions, I realized that I was questioning my own self as there was no answer. I turned back to find the answers to my queries.

The moment I turned, I was shocked. There was no one. The voice that had narrated the whole story to me was missing, the girl who came and tapped my shoulder was missing. The friend I made a while ago was invisible. How? Why? When? I was clueless.

How could that happen? I looked around in all directions but I couldn't see her. All I could feel was the story at the moment. It felt as if it gave me a tight hug.

That was perhaps one reason that after looking for her for a few more minutes, I decided to walk back with a story which had people who intrigued me no end. I wanted to meet them, I wanted to talk to them – to talk to the girl who had started influencing my mind to take decisions. Amaira was the name which revolved and rotated in my mind.

I kept thinking about Amaira, Kabir, Suhani and Kushank as I started to find my way. I thought, as I looked at the dew drops on the grass, 'Who was speaking?'

Was it Amaira, was it Suhani, or was it the story inside me? Was it the mind which was playing games or the supernatural that had a role in knitting the story. Well, I don't generally believe in all this but – was it...

Whatever it was, till I have a story in my head, I am a happy human being. And you?

Forthcoming by the same author

Imperfect Misfits

What if the heart stops listening to the mind? What if love stops adhering to rules and morals? And, what if love becomes more significant than its validation?

Tiasha and Shaurya have been friends for more than eight years, and in a relationship for three years. Nikhil has been with Sarah, his love interest, for the past five years. Everything looks rosy and perfect.

Until...

Tiasha meets Nikhil.

She meets him. Falls in love with his originality. Feelings accelerate.

And in the world of perfectly defined love, Tiasha becomes the imperfect addition, making life look like an *Imperfect Misfit*.

Will the much older Nikhil consider Tiasha's love? Will she ever be able to express her feelings? Will she ever be loved the way she was loved by Shaurya?

Join Tiasha as she struggles to sort the *Imperfect Misfits* that relationships have become.